CANDIDE
AND
L'INGÉNU

SIGNATURE EDITIONS

CANDIDE AND L'INGÉNU

VOLTAIRE

UNION SQUARE & CO.
NEW YORK

UNION SQUARE & CO. and the distinctive Union Square & Co. logo are trademarks of Sterling Publishing Co., Inc.

Union Square & Co., LLC, is a subsidiary of Sterling Publishing Co., Inc.

This 2025 edition published by Union Square & Co., LLC

A Note on the Text: These translations were originally published in 1918 (*Candide*) and 1768 (*L'Ingénu*) and reflect the attitudes of their time. The publisher's decision to present them as they were first published is not intended as endorsement of any offensive cultural representations or language.

ISBN 978-1-4549-5963-2
ISBN 978-1-4549-5964-9 (e-book)

For information about custom editions, special sales, and premium purchases, please contact specialsales@unionsquareandco.com.

Printed in India

2 4 6 8 10 9 7 5 3 1

unionsquareandco.com

Cover design by Igor Satanovsky and David Ter-Avanesyan
Cover images: *A Vase of Peonies, Chrysanthemums and a Carnation with Exotic Fruits in a Garden* by Jacobus Linthorst, courtesy of Artvee; Pavlo S/Shutterstock.com (icon)

CONTENTS

CANDIDE

CHAPTER I

How Candide Was Brought Up in a Fine Castle, and How He Was Expelled from Thence

THERE LIVED IN WESTPHALIA, IN THE CASTLE OF MY LORD THE Baron of Thunder-ten-tronckh, a young man, on whom nature had bestowed the most agreeable manners. His face was the index to his mind. He had an upright heart, with an easy frankness; which, I believe, was the reason he got the name of *Candide.* He was suspected, by the old servants of the family, to be the son of my Lord the Baron's sister, by a very honest gentleman of the neighborhood, whom the young lady declined to marry, because he could only produce seventy-one armorial quarterings; the rest of his genealogical tree having been destroyed through the injuries of time.

The Baron was one of the most powerful lords in Westphalia; his castle had both a gate and windows; and his great hall was even adorned with tapestry. The dogs of his outer yard composed his hunting pack upon occasion, his grooms were his huntsmen, and the vicar of the parish was his chief almoner. He was called My Lord by everybody, and everyone laughed when he told his stories.

My Lady the Baroness, who weighed about three hundred and fifty pounds, attracted, by that means, very great attention, and did the honors of the house with a dignity that rendered her still more respectable. Her daughter Cunegonde, aged about seventeen years, was of a ruddy complexion, fresh, plump, and well calculated to excite the passions. The Baron's son appeared to be in every respect worthy of his father. The preceptor, Pangloss, was the oracle of the house, and little Candide listened to his lectures with all the simplicity that was suitable to his age and character.

Pangloss taught metaphysico-theologo-cosmolonigology. He proved most admirably, that there could not be an effect without a cause; that, in this best of possible worlds, my Lord the Baron's castle was the most magnificent of castles, and my Lady the best of Baronesses that possibly could be.

"It is demonstrable," said he, "that things cannot be otherwise than they are: for all things having been made for some end, they must necessarily be for the best end. Observe well, that the nose has been made for carrying spectacles; therefore we have spectacles. The legs are visibly designed for stockings, and therefore we have stockings. Stones have been formed to be hewn, and make castles; therefore my Lord has a very fine castle; the greatest baron of the province ought to be the best accommodated. Swine were made to be eaten; therefore we eat pork all the year round: consequently, those who have merely asserted that all is good, have said a very foolish thing; they should have said all is the best possible."

Candide listened attentively, and believed implicitly; for he thought Miss Cunegonde extremely handsome, though he never had the courage to tell her so. He concluded, that next to the good fortune of being Baron of Thunder-ten-tronckh, the second degree of happiness was that of being Miss Cunegonde, the third to see her every day, and the fourth to listen to the teachings of Master Pangloss, the greatest philosopher of the province, and consequently of the whole world.

One day Cunegonde having taken a walk in the environs of the castle, in a little wood, which they called a park, espied Doctor Pangloss giving a lesson in experimental philosophy to her mother's chambermaid; a little brown wench, very handsome, and very docile. As Miss Cunegonde had a strong inclination for the sciences, she observed, without making any noise, the reiterated experiments that were going on before her eyes; she saw very clearly the sufficient reason of the Doctor, the effects and the causes; and she returned greatly flurried, quite pensive, and full of desire to be learned; imagining that she might be a sufficient reason for young Candide, who also, might be the same to her.

On her return to the castle, she met Candide, and blushed; Candide also blushed; she wished him good morrow with a faltering voice, and Candide answered her, hardly knowing what he said. The next day, after dinner, as they arose from table, Cunegonde and Candide happened to get behind the screen. Cunegonde dropped her handkerchief, and Candide picked it up; she, not thinking any harm, took hold of his hand; and the young man, not thinking any harm neither, kissed the hand of the young lady, with an eagerness, a sensibility, and grace, very particular; their lips met, their eyes sparkled, their knees trembled, their hands strayed.——The Baron of Thunder-ten-tronckh happening to pass close by the screen, and observing this cause and effect, thrust Candide out of the castle, with lusty kicks. Cunegonde fell into a swoon and as soon as she came to herself, was heartily cuffed on the ears by my Lady the Baroness. Thus all was thrown into confusion in the finest and most agreeable castle possible.

CHAPTER II

What Became of Candide Among the Bulgarians

CANDIDE BEING EXPELLED THE TERRESTRIAL PARADISE, RAMBLED a long while without knowing where, weeping, and lifting up his eyes to heaven, and sometimes turning them towards the finest of castles, which contained the handsomest of baronesses. He laid himself down, without his supper, in the open fields, between two furrows, while the snow fell in great flakes. Candide, almost frozen to death, crawled next morning to the neighboring village, which was called Waldber-ghoff-trarbk-dikdorff. Having no money, and almost dying with hunger and fatigue, he stopped in a dejected posture before the gate of an inn. Two men, dressed in blue, observing him in such a situation, "Brother," says one of them to the other, "there is a young fellow well built, and of a proper height." They accosted Candide, and invited him very civilly to dinner.

"Gentlemen," replied Candide, with an agreeable modesty, "you do me much honor, but I have no money to pay my shot."

"O sir," said one of the blues, "persons of your appearance and merit never pay anything; are you not five feet five inches high?"

"Yes, gentlemen, that is my height," returned he, making a bow.

"Come, sir, sit down at table; we will not only treat you, but we will never let such a man as you want money; men are made to assist one another."

"You are in the right," said Candide; "that is what Pangloss always told me, and I see plainly that everything is for the best."

They entreated him to take a few crowns, which he accepted, and would have given them his note; but they refused it, and sat down to table.

"Do not you tenderly love——?"

"O yes," replied he, "I tenderly love Miss Cunegonde."

"No," said one of the gentlemen; "we ask you if you do tenderly love the King of the Bulgarians?"

"Not at all," said he, "for I never saw him."

"How! he is the most charming of kings, and you must drink his health."

"O, with all my heart, gentlemen," and drinks.

"That is enough," said they to him; "you are now the bulwark, the support, the defender, the hero of the Bulgarians; your fortune is made, and you are certain of glory." Instantly they put him in irons, and carried him to the regiment. They made him turn to the right, to the left, draw the rammer, return the rammer, present, fire, step double; and they gave him thirty blows with a cudgel. The next day, he performed his exercises not quite so badly, and received but twenty blows; the third day the blows were restricted to ten, and he was looked upon by his fellow-soldiers, as a kind of prodigy.

Candide, quite stupefied, could not well conceive how he had become a hero. One fine Spring day he took it into his head to walk out, going straight forward, imagining that the human, as well as the animal species, were entitled to make whatever use they pleased of their limbs. He had not travelled two leagues, when four other heroes, six feet high, came up to him, bound him, and put him into a dungeon. He is asked by a Court-martial, whether he chooses to be whipped six and thirty times through the whole regiment, or receive at once twelve bullets through the forehead? He in vain argued that the will is free, and that he chose neither the one nor the other; he was obliged to make a choice; he therefore resolved, in virtue of God's gift called *free-will,* to run the gauntlet six and thirty times. He underwent this discipline twice. The regiment being composed of two thousand men, he received four thousand lashes, which laid open all his muscles and nerves, from the nape of the neck to the back. As they were proceeding to a third course, Candide, being quite spent, begged as a favor that they would be so kind as to shoot him; he obtained his request; they hoodwinked him, and made him kneel; the King of the Bulgarians passing by, inquired into the crime of the delinquent; and as this prince was a person of great penetration, he discovered from what he heard of Candide, that he was a young metaphysician, entirely ignorant of the things of this world; and he granted him his pardon, with a clemency which will be extolled in all histories, and throughout all ages. An experienced surgeon cured Candide in three weeks, with emollients prescribed by no less a master than Dioscorides. His skin had already began to grow again, and he was able to walk, when the King of the Bulgarians gave battle to the King of the Abares.

CHAPTER III

How Candide Made His Escape from the Bulgarians, and What Afterwards Befel Him

NOTHING COULD BE SO FINE, SO NEAT, SO BRILLIANT, SO WELL ordered, as the two armies. The trumpets, fifes, hautboys, drums, and cannon, formed an harmony superior to what hell itself could invent. The cannon swept off at first about six thousand men on each side; afterwards, the musketry carried away from the best of worlds, about nine or ten thousand rascals that infected its surface. The bayonet was likewise the sufficient reason of the death of some thousands of men. The whole number might amount to about thirty thousand souls. Candide, who trembled like a philosopher, hid himself as well as he could, during this heroic butchery.

At last, while each of the two kings were causing *Te Deum*—glory to God—to be sung in their respective camps, he resolved to go somewhere else, to reason upon the effects and causes. He walked over heaps of the dead and dying; he came at first to a neighboring village belonging to the Abares, but found it in ashes; for it had been burnt by the Bulgarians, according to the law of nations. Here were to be seen old men full of wounds, casting their eyes on their murdered wives, who were holding their infants to their bloody breasts. You might see in another place, virgins outraged after they had satisfied the natural desires of some of those heroes, whilst breathing out their last sighs. Others, half-burnt, praying earnestly for instant death. The whole field was covered with brains, and with legs and arms lopped off.

Candide betook himself with all speed to another village. It belonged to the Bulgarians, and had met with the same treatment from the Abarian heroes. Candide, walking still forward over quivering limbs, or through rubbish of houses, got at last out of the theatre of war, having some small quantity of provisions in his knapsack, and never forgetting Miss Cunegonde. His provisions failed him when he arrived in Holland; but having heard that every one was rich in that country, and that they were Christians, he did not doubt but he should be as well treated there as he had been in my Lord the Baron's castle, before he had been expelled thence on account of Miss Cunegonde's sparkling eyes.

He asked alms from several grave-looking persons, who all replied, that if he continued that trade, they would confine him in a house of correction, where he should learn to earn his bread.

He applied afterwards to a man, who for a whole hour had been discoursing on the subject of charity, before a large assembly. This orator, looking at him askance, said to him:

"What are you doing here? are you for the good cause?"

"There is no effect without a cause," replied Candide, modestly; "all is necessarily linked, and ordered for the best. A necessity banished me from Miss Cunegonde; a necessity forced me to run the gauntlet; another necessity makes me beg my bread, till I can get into some business by which to earn it. All this could not be otherwise."

"My friend," said the orator to him, "do you believe that the Anti-Christ is alive?"

"I never heard whether he is or not," replied Candide; "but whether he is, or is not, I want bread!"

"You do not deserve to eat any," said the other; "get you gone, you rogue; get you gone, you wretch; never in thy life come near me again!"

The orator's wife, having popped her head out of the chamber window, and seeing a man who doubted whether Anti-Christ was alive, poured on his head a full vessel of dirty water. Oh heavens! to what excess does religious zeal transport the fair sex!

A man who had not been baptized, a good Anabaptist, named *James,* saw the barbarous and ignominious manner with which they treated one of his brethren, a being with two feet, without feathers, and endowed with a rational soul. He took him home with him, cleaned him, gave him bread and beer, made him a present of two florins, and offered to teach him the method of working in his manufactories of Persian stuffs, which are fabricated in Holland. Candide, prostrating himself almost to the ground, cried out, "Master Pangloss argued well when he said, that everything is for the best in this world; for I am infinitely more affected with your very great generosity, than by the hard-heartedness of that gentleman with the cloak, and the lady his wife."

Next day, as he was taking a walk, he met a beggar, all covered over with sores, his eyes half dead, the tip of his nose eaten off, his mouth turned to one side of his face, his teeth black, speaking through his throat, tormented with a violent cough, with gums so rotten, that his teeth came near falling out every time he spit.

CHAPTER IV

How Candide Met His Old Master of Philosophy, Dr. Pangloss, and What Happened to Them

CANDIDE MOVED STILL MORE WITH COMPASSION THAN WITH horror, gave this frightful mendicant the two florins which he had received of his honest Anabaptist James. The spectre fixed his eyes attentively upon him, dropped some tears, and was going to fall upon his neck. Candide, affrighted, drew back.

"Alas!" said the one wretch to the other, "don't you know your dear Pangloss?"

"What do I hear! Is it you, my dear master! you in this dreadful condition! What misfortune has befallen you? Why are you no longer in the most magnificent of castles? What has become of Miss Cunegonde, the nonpareil of the fair sex, the masterpiece of nature?"

"I have no more strength," said Pangloss.

Candide immediately carried him to the Anabaptist's stable, where he gave him a little bread to eat. When Pangloss was refreshed a little, "Well," said Candide, "what has become of Cunegonde?"

"She is dead," replied the other.

Candide fainted away at this word; but his friend recovered his senses, with a little bad vinegar which he found by chance in the stable.

Candide opening his eyes, cried out, "Cunegonde is dead! Ah, best of worlds, where art thou now? But of what distemper did she die? Was not the cause, her seeing me driven out of the castle by my Lord, her father, with such hard kicks on the breech?"

"No," said Pangloss, "she was gutted by some Bulgarian soldiers, after having been barbarously ravished. They knocked my Lord the Baron on the head, for attempting to protect her; my Lady the Baroness was cut in pieces; my poor pupil was treated like his sister; and as for the castle, there is not one stone left upon another, nor a barn, nor a sheep, nor a duck, nor a tree. But we have been sufficiently revenged; for the Abarians have done the very same thing to a neighboring barony, which belonged to a Bulgarian Lord."

At this discourse, Candide fainted away a second time; but coming to himself, and having said all that he ought to say, he inquired into the cause and the effect, and into the sufficient reason that had reduced Pangloss to so deplorable a condition. "Alas," said the other, "it was love; love, the comforter of the human race, the preserver of the universe, the soul of all sensible beings, tender love." "Alas!" said Candide, "I know this love, the sovereign of hearts, the soul of our soul; yet it never cost me more than a kiss, and twenty kicks. But how could this charming cause produce in you so abominable an effect?"

Pangloss made answer as follows: "Oh my dear Candide, you knew Paquetta, the pretty attendant on our noble Baroness; I tasted in her arms the delights of Paradise, which produced those torments of hell with which you see me devoured. She was infected, and perhaps she is dead. Paquetta received this present from a very learned cavalier, who had it from an old countess, who received it from a captain of horse, who was indebted for it to a marchioness, who got it from a Spaniard. For my part, I shall give it to nobody, for I am dying."

"Oh Pangloss!" cried Candide, "what a strange genealogy! Was not the devil at the head of it?" "Not at all," replied the great man; "it was a thing indispensable; a necessary ingredient in the best of worlds; for if the Spaniard had not catched, in an island of America, this distemper, we should have had neither chocolate nor cochineal. It may also be observed, that to this day, upon our continent, this malady is as peculiar to us, as is religious controversy. The Turks, the Indians, the Persians, the Chinese, the Siamese, and the Japanese, know nothing of it yet. But there is sufficient reason why they, in their turn, should become acquainted with it, a few centuries hence. In the meantime, it has made marvellous progress among us, and especially in those great armies composed of honest hirelings, well disciplined, who decide the fate of states; for we may rest assured, that when thirty thousand men in a pitched battle fight against troops equal to them in number, there are about twenty thousand of them on each side who have the pox."

"That is admirable," said Candide; "but you must be cured." "Ah! how can I?" said Pangloss; "I have not a penny, my friend; and throughout the whole extent of this globe, we cannot get anyone to bleed us, or give us a glister, without paying for it, or getting some other person to pay for us."

This last speech determined Candide. He went and threw himself at the feet of his charitable Anabaptist James, and gave him so touching a description of the state his friend was reduced to, that the good man did not hesitate to entertain Dr. Pangloss, and he had him cured at his own expense. During the cure, Pangloss lost only an eye and an ear. As he wrote well, and understood arithmetic perfectly, the Anabaptist made him his bookkeeper. At the end of two months, being obliged to go to Lisbon on account of his business, he took the two philosophers along with him, in his ship. Pangloss explained to him how everything was such as it could not be better; but James was not of this opinion. "Mankind," said he, "must have somewhat corrupted their nature; for they were not born wolves, and yet they have become wolves; God has given them neither cannon of twenty-four pounds, nor bayonets; and yet they have made cannon and bayonets to destroy one another, I might throw into the account bankrupts; and the law which seizes on the effects of bankrupts only to bilk the creditors." "All this was indispensable," replied the one-eyed doctor, "and private misfortunes constitute the general good; so that the more private misfortunes there are, the whole is the better." While he was thus reasoning, the air grew dark, the winds blew from the four quarters of the world, and the ship was attacked by a dreadful storm, within sight of the harbor of Lisbon.

CHAPTER V

Tempest, Shipwreck, Earthquake, and What Became of Dr. Pangloss, Candide, and James the Anabaptist

ONE HALF OF THE PASSENGERS BEING WEAKENED, AND READY TO breathe their last, with the inconceivable anguish which the rolling of the ship conveyed through the nerves and all the humors of the body, which were quite disordered, were not capable of being alarmed at the danger they were in. The other half uttered cries and made prayers; the sails were rent, the masts broken, and the ship became leaky. Everyone worked that was able, nobody cared for anything, and no order was kept. The Anabaptist contributed his assistance to work the ship. As he was upon deck, a furious sailor rudely struck him, and laid him sprawling on the planks; but with the blow he gave him, he himself was so violently jolted, that he tumbled overboard with his head foremost, and remained suspended by a piece of a broken mast. Honest James ran to his assistance, and helped him on deck again; but in the attempt, he fell into the sea, in the sight of the sailor, who suffered him to perish, without deigning to look upon him. Candide drew near and saw his benefactor, one moment emerging, and the next swallowed up for ever. He was just going to throw himself into the sea after him, when the philosopher Pangloss hindered him, by demonstrating to him, that the road to Lisbon had been made on purpose for this Anabaptist to be drowned in. While he was proving this, *a priori*, the vessel foundered, and all perished except Pangloss, Candide, and the brutal sailor, who drowned the virtuous

Anabaptist. The villain luckily swam ashore, whither Pangloss and Candide were carried on a plank.

When they had recovered themselves a little, they walked towards Lisbon. They had some money left, with which they hoped to save themselves from hunger, after having escaped from the storm.

Scarce had they set foot in the city, bewailing the death of their benefactor, when they perceived the earth to tremble under their feet, and saw the sea swell in the harbor, and dash to pieces the ships that were at anchor. The whirling flames and ashes covered the streets and public places, the houses tottered, and their roofs fell to the foundations, and the foundations were scattered; thirty thousand inhabitants of all ages and sexes were crushed to death in the ruins. The sailor, whistling and swearing, said, "There is some booty to be got here." "What can be the sufficient reason of this phenomenon?" said Pangloss. "This is certainly the last day of the world," cried Candide. The sailor ran quickly into the midst of the ruins, encountered death to find money, found it, laid hold of it, got drunk, and having slept himself sober, purchased the favors of the first willing girl he met with, among the ruins of the demolished houses, and in the midst of the dying and the dead. While he was thus engaged, Pangloss pulled him by the sleeve; "My friend," said he, "this is not right; you trespass against universal reason, you choose your time badly." "Brains and blood!" answered the other; "I am a sailor, and was born at Batavia; you have mistaken your man, this time, with your universal reason."

Some pieces of stone having wounded Candide, he lay sprawling in the street, and covered with rubbish. "Alas!" said he to Pangloss, "get me a little wine and oil; I am dying." "This trembling of the earth is no new thing," answered Pangloss. The City of Lima, in America, experienced the same concussions last year; the same cause has the same effects; there is certainly a train of sulphur under the earth, from Lima to Lisbon." "Nothing is more probable," said Candide; "but, for God's sake, a little oil and wine." "How probable?" replied the philosopher; "I maintain that the thing is demonstrable." Candide lost all sense, and Pangloss brought him a little water from a neighbouring fountain.

The day following, having found some provisions, in rummaging through the rubbish, they recruited their strength a little. Afterwards, they employed themselves like others, in administering relief to the inhabitants that had escaped from death. Some citizens that had been relieved by them, gave them as good a dinner as could be expected amidst such a disaster. It is true that the repast was mournful, and the guests watered their bread with their tears. But Pangloss consoled them by the assurance that things could not be otherwise; "For," said he, "all this must necessarily be for the best. As this volcano is at Lisbon, it could not be elsewhere; as it is impossible that things should not be what they are, as all is good."

A little man clad in black, who belonged to the inquisition, and sat at his side, took him up very politely, and said: "It seems, sir, you do not believe in original sin; for if all is for the best, then there has been neither fall nor punishment."

"I most humbly ask your excellency's pardon," answered Pangloss, still more politely; "for the fall of man and the curse necessarily entered into the best of worlds possible." "Then, sir, you do not believe there is liberty," said the inquisitor. "Your Excellency will excuse me," said Pangloss; "liberty can consist with absolute necessity; for it was necessary we should be free; because, in short, the determinate will——"

Pangloss was in the middle of his proposition, when the inquisitor made a signal with his head to the tall armed footman in a cloak, who waited upon him, to bring him a glass of port wine.

CHAPTER VI

How a Fine Inquisition Was Celebrated to Prevent Earthquakes, and How Candide Was Whipped

After the earthquake, which had destroyed three-fourths of Lisbon, the sages of the country could not find any means more effectual to prevent a total destruction, than to give the people a splendid inquisition. It had been decided by the university of Coimbra, that the spectacle of some persons burnt to death by a slow fire, with great ceremony, was an infallible antidote for earthquakes.

In consequence of this resolution, they had seized a Biscayan, convicted of having married his godmother, and two Portuguese, who, in eating a pullet, had stripped off the lard. After dinner, they came and secured Dr. Pangloss, and his disciple Candide; the one for having spoke too freely, and the other for having heard with an air of approbation. They were both conducted to separate apartments, extremely damp, and never incommoded with the sun. Eight days after, they were both clothed with a gown and had their heads—adorned with paper crowns. Candide's crown and gown were painted with inverted flames, and with devils that had neither tails nor claws; but Pangloss's devils had claws and tails, and the flames were pointed upwards. Being thus dressed, they marched in procession, and heard a very pathetic speech followed by fine music on a squeaking organ. Candide was whipped on the back in cadence, while they were singing; the Biscayan, and the two men who would not eat lard, were burnt;

and Pangloss, though it was contrary to custom, was hanged. The same day, the earth shook anew, with a most dreadful noise.

Candide, affrighted, interdicted, astonished, all bloody, all panting, said to himself: "If this is the best of possible worlds, what then are the rest? Supposing I had not been whipped now, I have been so, among the Bulgarians; but, Oh, my dear Pangloss; thou greatest of philosophers, that it should be my fate to see thee hanged without knowing for what! Oh! my dear Anabaptist! thou best of men, that it should be thy fate to be drowned in the harbor! Oh! Miss Cunegonde! the jewel of ladies, that it should be thy fate to have been outraged and slain!"

He returned, with difficulty, supporting himself, after being lectured, whipped, absolved, and blessed, when an old woman accosted him, and said: "Child, take courage, and follow me."

CHAPTER VII

How an Old Woman Took Care of Candide, and How He Found the Object He Loved

Candide did not take courage, but he followed the old woman to a ruinated house. She gave him a pot of pomatum to anoint himself, left him something to eat and drink, and showed him a very neat little bed, near which was a complete suit of clothes. "Eat, drink, and sleep," said she to him, "and may God take care of you. I will be back to-morrow." Candide, astonished at all he had seen, at all he had suffered, and still more at the charity of the old woman, offered to kiss her hand. "You must not kiss my hand," said the old woman. "I will be back to-morrow. Rub yourself with the pomatum, eat and take rest."

Candide, notwithstanding so many misfortunes, ate, and went to sleep. Next morning, the old woman brought him his breakfast, looked at his back, and rubbed it herself with another ointment; she afterwards brought him his dinner; and she returned at night, and brought him his supper. The day following she performed the same ceremonies. "Who are you?" would Candide always say to her; "Who has inspired you with so much goodness? What thanks can I render you?" The good woman made no answer; she returned in the evening, but brought him no supper. "Come along with me," said he, "and say not a word." She took him by the arm, and walked with him into the country about a quarter of a mile; they arrived at a house that stood by itself, surrounded with gardens and canals. The old woman knocked at a little door, which being opened, she conducted Candide by a private stair-case into a gilded closet, and leaving him on a brocade couch, shut the door and went her way. Candide thought he was in a revery, and looked upon all his life as an unlucky dream, but at the present moment, a very agreeable vision.

The old woman returned very soon, supporting with difficulty a woman trembling, of a majestic port, glittering with jewels, and covered with a veil. "Take off that veil," said the old woman to Candide. The young man approached and took off the veil with a trembling hand. What joy! what surprise! he thought he saw Miss Cunegonde; he saw her indeed! it was she herself. His strength failed him, he could not utter a word, but fell down at her feet. Cunegonde fell upon the carpet. The old woman applied aromatic waters; they recovered their senses, and spoke to one another. At first, their words were broken, their questions and answers crossed each other, amidst sighs, tears, and cries. The old woman recommended them to make less noise, and then left them to themselves. "How! is it you?" said Candide; "are you still alive? do I find you again in Portugal? You were not ravished then, as the philosopher Pangloss assured me?" "Yes, all this was so," said the lovely Cunegonde; "but death does not always follow from these two accidents." "But your father and mother! were they not killed?" "It is but too true," answered Cunegonde, weeping. "And your brother?" "My brother was killed too." "And why are you in Portugal? and how did you know that I was here? and by what strange adventure did you contrive to bring me to this house?" "I will tell you all that, presently," replied the lady; "but first you must inform me of all that has happened to you, since the harmless kiss you gave me, and the rude kicking which you received for it."

Candide obeyed her with the most profound respect; and though he was forbidden to speak, though his voice was weak and faltering, and though his back still pained him, yet he related to her, in the most artless manner, everything that had befallen him since the moment of their separation. Cunegonde lifted up her eyes to heaven; she shed tears at the death of the good Anabaptist, and of Pangloss; after which she thus related her adventures to Candide, who lost not a word, but looked on her, as if he would devour her with his eyes.

CHAPTER VIII

The History of Cunegonde

"I WAS IN MY BED AND FAST ASLEEP, WHEN IT PLEASED HEAVEN TO send the Bulgarians to our fine castle of Thunder-ten-tronckh; they murdered my father and my brother, and cut my mother to pieces. A huge Bulgarian, six feet high, perceiving the horrible sight had deprived me of my senses, set himself to ravish me. This abuse made me come to myself; I recovered my senses, I cried, I struggled, I bit, I scratched, I wanted to tear out the huge Bulgarian's eyes, not considering that what had happened in my father's castle, was a common thing in war. The brute gave me a cut with his hanger, the mark of which I still bear about me." "Ah! I anxiously wish to see it," said the simple Candide. "You shall," answered Cunegonde; but let me finish my story." "Do so," replied Candide.

She then resumed the thread of her story, as follows: "A Bulgarian captain came in, and saw me bleeding; but the soldier was not at all disconcerted. The Captain flew into a passion at the little respect the brute showed him, and killed him upon my body. He then caused me to be dressed, and carried me as a prisoner of war to his own quarters. I washed the scanty linen he had, and cooked his victuals. He found me very pretty, I must say it; and I cannot deny but he was well shaped, and that he had a white, soft skin; but for the rest, he had little sense or philosophy; one could plainly see that he was not bred under Dr. Pangloss.

At the end of three months, having lost all his money, and being grown out of conceit with me, he sold me to a Jew, named *Don Issachar,* who traded to Holland and Portugal, and had a most violent passion for women. This Jew laid close siege to my person, but could not triumph over me; I have resisted him better than I did the Bulgarian soldier. A woman of honor may be ravished once, but her virtue gathers strength from such rudeness. The Jew, in order to render me more tractable, brought me to this country-house that you see. I always imagined hitherto, that no place on earth was so fine as the castle of Thunder-ten-tronckh; but I am now undeceived.

"The grand inquisitor observing me one day ogled me very strongly, and sent me a note, saying he wanted to speak with me upon private business. Being conducted to his palace, I informed him of my birth; upon which he represented to me, how much it was below my family to belong to an Israelite. A proposal was then made by him to Don Issachar, to yield me up to my Lord. But Don Issachar, who is the court-banker, and a man of credit, would not come into his measures. The inquisitor threatened him. At last, my Jew, being affrighted, concluded a bargain, by which the house and myself should belong to them both in common; the Jew to have possession Monday, Friday, and Saturday, and the inquisitor, the other days of the week. This agreement has now continued six months. It has not, however, been without quarrels; for it has been often disputed whether Saturday night or Sunday belonged to the old, or to the new law. For my part, I have hitherto disagreed with them both; and I believe that this is the reason I am still beloved by them.

"At length, to avert the scourge of earthquakes and to intimidate Don Issachar, it pleased his Lordship the inquisitor to celebrate. He did me the honor to invite me to it. I got a very fine seat, and the ladies were served with refreshments between the ceremonies. I was seized with horror at seeing them burn the two Jews, and the honest Biscayan who married his godmother; but how great was my surprise, my consternation, my anguish, when I saw in a sanbenito and mitre, a person that somewhat resembled

Pangloss! I rubbed my eyes, I looked upon him very attentively, and I saw him hanged. I fell into a swoon, and scarce had I recovered my senses, when I saw you stripped stark naked; this was the height of horror, consternation, grief, and despair. I will frankly own to you, that your skin is still whiter, and of a better complexion then that of my Bulgarian captain. This sight increased all the sensations that oppressed and distracted my soul. I cried out, I was going to say stop, barbarians; but my voice failed me, and all my cries would have been to no purpose. When you had been severely whipped: How is it possible, said I, that the amiable Candide, and the sage Pangloss, should both be at Lisbon;—the one to receive a hundred lashes and the other to be hanged by order of my Lord the Inquisitor, by whom I am so greatly beloved? Pangloss certainly deceived me most cruelly, when he said that everything was for the best in this world.

"Agitated, astonished, sometimes beside myself, and sometimes ready to die with weakness; my head filled with the massacre of my father, my mother, and my brother, the insolence of the vile Bulgarian soldier, the stab he gave me with his hanger, my abject servitude, and my acting as cook to the Bulgarian captain; the rascal Don Issachar, my abominable inquisitor, the execution of Dr. Pangloss, the grand music on the organ while you were whipped, and especially the kiss I gave you behind the screen, the last day I saw you. I praised the Lord for having restored you to me after so many trials. I charged my old woman to take care of you, and to bring you hither as soon as she could. She has executed her commission very well; I have tasted the inexpressible pleasure of seeing you, hearing you, and speaking to you. You must have a ravenous appetite, by this time; I am hungry myself, too; let us therefore, sit down to supper."

On this, they both sat down to table; and after supper, they seated themselves on the fine couch before mentioned. They were there, when Signor Don Issachar, one of the masters of the house, came in. It was his Sabbath day, and he came to enjoy his right, and to express his tender love.

CHAPTER IX

What Happened to Cunegonde, Candide, the Grand Inquisitor, and the Jew

THIS ISSACHAR WAS THE MOST CHOLERIC HEBREW THAT HAD been seen in Israel since the captivity in Babylon. "What," said he, "you dog of a Galilean, is it not enough to share with Monsieur the inquisitor? but must this varlet also share with me?" When he had thus spoke, he drew out a long poniard, which he always carried about him, and not suspecting that his antagonist had any weapons, he fell upon Candide; but our honest Westphalian had received a fine sword from the old woman, along with his full suit. He drew his rapier, and in spite of his amiable temper, he laid the Israelite dead upon the spot, at the feet of Cunegonde.

"My God," cried she; "What will become of us? a man murdered in my apartment! If the peace-officer comes in, we are ruined." "If Pangloss had not been hanged," said Candide, "he would have given us excellent advice in this emergency; for he was a great philosopher. In this extremity, let us consult the old woman"—She was a very prudent woman, and began to give her advice, when another little door opened. It was now about one o'clock in the morning, and consequently the beginning of Sunday. This day was allotted to my Lord the inquisitor. Entering, he saw the kicked Candide with a sword in his hand, a dead body stretched on the floor, Cunegonde in a dreadful fright, and the old woman giving advice.

See now what passed in Candide's mind at this instant, and how he reasoned: "If this holy man calls in assistance, he will infallibly have me roasted alive; he may treat Cunegonde in the same manner; he has caused me to be whipped without mercy; he is my rival; I am already in for manslaughter; there is no time to hesitate." This reasoning was clear and rapid; and without giving time to the inquisitor to recover from his surprise, he ran through the body, and laid him by the side of the Jew. "Behold, a second killed!" said Cunegonde; "there is no pardon for us; we are damned, our last hour is come. How could you, who are so very gentle, kill a Jew and a lord in two minutes time?" "My fair Lady," answered Candide, "when a man is in love, jealous, and has been whipped by the inquisition, he does not know what he does."

The old woman then put in her word, and said, "There are three Andalusian horses in the stable, with their saddles and bridles; which the gallant Candide may get ready; Madam has some money and jewels; let us get on horseback without delay, and let us go to Cadiz; the weather is delightful, and very pleasant it is to travel in the cool of night."

Candide immediately saddled the three horses. Cunegonde, the old woman, and he, travelled thirty miles on a stretch. While they were making the best of their way, the citizenry came to the house; they buried my Lord in a magnificent church, and threw Issachar into a common sewer.

Candide, Cunegonde, and the old woman, had now got to the little town of Avacena, in the middle of the mountains of Sierra Morena; having put up at an inn, they talked on affairs as follows.

CHAPTER X

In What Distress Candide, Cunegonde, and the Old Woman Arrived at Cadiz and of Their Embarkation

"WHO COULD HAVE ROBBED ME OF MY PISTOLES AND MY DIAMONDS?" said Cunegonde, with tears in her eyes; "what shall we live on? what shall we do? where shall I find inquisitors and Jews to give me more money and jewels?" "Alas," said the old woman, "I strongly suspect a cavalier who slept yesterday in the same inn with us at Badajos. God preserve me from judging rashly, but he came twice into our chamber, and went away a long time before us." "Ah!" said Candide, "the good Pangloss has often demonstrated to me, that the goods of this world are common to all men, and that everyone has an equal right to them. According to these principles, the cavalier ought to have left us enough to carry us to our journey's end. Have you nothing at all left then, my pretty Cunegonde?" "Not a farthing," said she. "What course shall we take?" said Candide. "Let us sell one of the horses," said the old woman; "I can ride behind Miss, and we shall thus manage to reach Cadiz."

In the same inn was a Benedictine prior, who bought the horse very cheap. Candide, Cunegonde, and the old woman, passed through Lucena, Chillas, and Lebrixa and arrived at length at Cadiz, where they were fitting out a fleet, and assembling troops for bringing to reason the reverend fathers, the Jesuits of Parragua, who were accused of having excited one of their hordes, near the city of St. Sacrament, to revolt from their allegiance to the Kings of Spain and Portugal. Candide having served among the Bulgarians, performed the military exercise of that nation before the commander of this little army, with so much grace, celerity, address, dexterity, and agility, that he gave him command of a company of infantry. Being now made a captain, he embarked with Miss Cunegonde, the old woman, two valets, and the two Andalusian horses, which had belonged to his Lordship, the grand Inquisitor of Portugal.

During the whole voyage, they argued a great deal on the philosophy of poor Pangloss. "We are going to another world," said Candide; "it is there, without doubt, that every thing is for the best. For it must be confessed, that one has reason to be a little uneasy at what passes in this world, with respect to both physics and morals." "I love you with all my heart," said Cunegonde, "but my mind is still terrified at what I have seen and experienced." "All will be well," replied Candide; "the seas of the new world are preferable to those of Europe; they are more calm and the winds are more constant. Certainly, the new world is the best of all possible worlds."

"God grant it," said Cunegonde; "but I have been so terribly unfortunate here, that my heart is almost shut up against hope." "You complain, indeed," said the old woman; "alas! you have not met with such misfortunes as I have."

Cunegonde was almost ready to fall a laughing, and thought the old woman very comical, for pretending to be more unfortunate than herself.

"Alas, my good dame," said Cunegonde; "unless you have been ravished by two Bulgarians, and received two cuts with a hanger and had two castles demolished, and had two fathers and two mothers murdered, and have seen two lovers whipped, I cannot see how you can have the advantage of me. Add to this, that I was born a baroness, with seventy-two armorial quarterings, and that I have, nevertheless, been a cook-maid." "My Lady," answered the old woman, "you know nothing of my ancestry, and were I to show you my back, you would not talk as you do, but would suspend your judgment." This discourse having raised an insatiable curiosity in the minds of Cunegonde and Candide, the old woman related her story as follows.

CHAPTER XI

The History of the Old Woman

My eyes have not always been bleared, and bordered with scarlet; my nose has not always touched my chin; nor have I been always a servant. I am the daughter of a king, and the Princess of Palestrina. I was brought up, till I was fourteen, in a palace, to which all the castles of your German barons would not have served for stables, and one of my robes cost more than all the magnificence in Westphalia. I increased in beauty, in charms, and in fine accomplishments, amidst pleasures, homages, and high expectations. I began to captivate every heart. My neck was formed—oh, what a neck! white, firm, and shaped like that of the Venus de Medici. And what eyes; what eyelids! what fine black eyebrows! what flames sparkled from my eyeballs; the poets of my country told me they eclipsed the twinkling of the stars! The maids who dressed and undressed me fell into an ecstasy when they viewed me, and all the men would gladly have been in their places.

I was betrothed to a prince, the sovereign of Massa Carara. What a prince! as handsome as myself, all sweetness and charms, of a witty mind, and burning with love. I loved him, as one always loves for the first time, with idolatry, with transport. Preparations were made for our nuptials. The pomp and magnificence were inconceivable; nothing but continual feasts, carousals, and operas; and all Italy made sonnets upon me, of which there was scarce one tolerable. I was just on the point of reaching the summit of happiness, when an old marchioness, who had been mistress to my prince, invited him to drink chocolate at her house. He died there in less than two hours time in terrible convulsions. But this is only a mere trifle. My mother, in despair, and yet less afflicted than I was, resolved to retreat for some time from so mournful a place. She had a very fine country-seat near Gaeta. We embarked on board a galley of the country, gilt equal to the altar of St. Peter at Rome. We were scarcely at sea, when a corsair of Sallee fell upon and boarded us. Our soldiers defended themselves like true soldiers; they all fell upon their knees, after throwing away their arms, and asked pardon, *in articulo mortis,* of the corsair.

We were instantly stripped naked as monkeys; my mother, our maids of honor, and myself too, meeting with no better usage. It is a very surprising thing with what expedition these pirate gentry undress people. But what surprised me most was, that they should touch us where we women do not ordinarily allow. This ceremony appeared very strange to me; but so we judge of everything that is not done in our own country. I soon learned, that the search was to find out whether we had not concealed some of our jewels there. It is a custom established time out of mind among civilized nations that scour the sea. I know that those gentlemen, the pious knights of Malta, never omit to practice it, when they capture Turks of either sex. It is one of the laws of nations, from which they never deviate.

I need not tell you how great a hardship it is for a young princess and her mother to be carried slaves to Morocco. You may easily form a notion of what we underwent on board the vessel of the corsair. My mother was still very handsome; our maids of honor, nay, our plain chambermaids, had more charms than are to be found throughout all Africa. As for myself, I was all attraction, I was all beauty, and all charms; nay, more, I was a virgin. However, I was not one long; this flower, which had been reserved for the accomplished Prince of Massa Carara, was taken from me by the captain of the corsair. He was an ugly negro, but fancied he did me a great deal of honor. Indeed her Highness, the Princess of Palestrina and myself, must have been very strong to resist all the violence we met with till our arrival at Morocco. But let me pass over that; these things are so very common that they are hardly worth the mentioning.

Morocco overflowed with blood when we arrived there. Fifty sons of the Emperor Muley Ismael had each their adherents; this produced, in effect, fifty civil wars, of blacks against blacks, of blacks against tawnies, of tawnies against tawnies, and of mulattoes against mulattoes. In a word, there was one continued carnage all over the empire.

No sooner were we landed than the blacks of a party adverse to that of my corsair made an attempt to rob him of his booty. Next to the jewels and the gold, we were the most valuable things he had. I was here witness to such a battle as you never saw in your European climates. The people of the north have not so much fire in their blood, nor have they that raging passion for women that is so common in Africa. One would think that you Europeans had nothing but milk in your veins; but it is vitriol and fire that runs in those of the inhabitants of Mount Atlas and the neighboring countries. They fought with the fury of lions, tigers, and serpents of the country, to determine who should have us. A Moor seized my mother by the right arm, while my captain's lieutenant held her by the left; a Moorish soldier took hold of her by one leg, and our pirates held her by the other. All our women found themselves almost in a moment seized thus by four soldiers. My captain kept me concealed at his back. He had a scimitar in his hand, and killed everyone that opposed his fury. In short, I saw all our Italian women and my mother torn in pieces, hacked and mangled by the brutes that fought for them. My fellow-prisoners, those who had taken them, soldiers, sailors, blacks, whites, mulattoes, and lastly my captain himself, were all killed; and I remained expiring upon a heap of dead bodies. These barbarous scenes extended, as everyone knows, over more than three hundred leagues, without the perpetrators ever omitting the five prayers a day ordained by Mahomet.

I disengaged myself with great difficulty from the weight of so many dead, bloody carcases heaped upon me, and made shift to crawl to a large orange-tree on the bank of a neighboring rivulet, where I sank down oppressed with fear, fatigue, horror, despair, and hunger. Soon after, my senses being overpowered, I fell into a sleep, which resembled a fainting fit rather than sleep. I was in this state of weakness and insensibility, between death and life, when I felt myself pressed by something that moved near my body. I opened my eyes, and saw a white man of a very good mien, who sighed, and muttered between his teeth in my own speech.

CHAPTER XII

The Sequel of the Old Woman's Adventures

Astonished, and transported with joy, to hear my own country language, I roused myself and determined to relate the great misfortunes that had befallen me. I then gave him a short account of the horrid scenes I had undergone, and relapsed again into a swoon. He carried me to a neighboring house, caused me to be put to bed, gave me something to eat, waited upon me, comforted and flattered me, and said that he had never seen anyone so handsome as I was. "I was born at Naples," said he, "where they castrate two or three thousand children every year; some die of the operation, others acquire a finer voice than that of any woman, and others become governors of states. This operation was performed on me with great success, and I became a singer in the chapel of her Highness, the Princess of Palestrina." "Of my mother!" cried I. "Of your mother?" cried he again, shedding tears. "What! are you that young princess, whom I had the care of bringing up till she was six years old, and who bid fair, even then, to be as handsome as you are now?" "It is myself; my mother lies about four hundred paces from hence, cut into four quarters, under a heap of dead bodies."

I related to him all that had befallen me; he likewise told me his adventures, and informed me that he was sent to the King of Morocco, by a Christian prince, to conclude a treaty with that monarch, by which he was to furnish him with ammunition, artillery, and ships, to enable him entirely to destroy the commerce of other Christians. "My commission is fulfilled," said the honest eunuch to me; "I am going to embark at Ceuta, and will carry you to Italy."

I thanked him with tears of gratitude; but instead of conducting me to Italy, he carried me to Algiers, and sold me to the Dey of that province. Scarce was I sold, when the plague, which had made the tour of Africa, Asia, and Europe, broke out at Algiers with great fury. You have seen earthquakes; but pray, Miss, have you ever had the plague! "Never," answered the Baroness.

"Had you had it," replied the old woman, "you would confess that it is far more terrible than an earthquake." It is very common in Africa; I was seized with it. Figure to yourself the situation of a king's daughter, about fifteen years of age, who, in the space of three months, had undergone poverty and slavery, had been ravished almost every day, had seen her mother cut into four quarters, had experienced both famine and war, and was dying of the plague at Algiers. I did not die for all that. But my eunuch, and the Dey, and almost all the seraglio at Algiers, perished.

When the first ravages of this dreadful pestilence were over, they sold the slaves belonging to the Dey. A merchant purchased me, and carried me to Tunis. There he sold me to another merchant, who sold me again at Tripoli; from Tripoli, I was sold again at Alexandria; from Alexandria, I was sold again at Smyrna; and from Smyrna at Constantinople. At last, I became the property of an Aga of the Janissaries, who was soon after ordered to go to the defence of Asoph, then besieged by the Russians.

The Aga, who was a man of great gallantry, took all his seraglio along with him, and lodged us in a small fort on the Palus Maeotis, under the guard of two black eunuchs and twenty soldiers. We killed a great number of the Russians, who returned the compliment with interest. Asoph was put to fire and sword, and no regard was paid to age or sex. There remained only our little fort, which the enemy resolved to reduce by famine. The twenty Janissaries had sworn that they would never surrender. The extremities of famine to which they were reduced, obliged them to eat our two eunuchs, for fear of violating their oath; and a few days after, they resolved to devour the women.

We had an Iman, a very religious and humane man. He preached an excellent sermon to them, in which he dissuaded them from killing us all at once. "Cut off only one of the backs of these ladies," said he, "and you will fare excellently well; if you must come to it again, you will have the same entertainment a few days hence. Heaven will bless you for so charitable an action, and you will find relief."

As he had an eloquent tongue, he easily persuaded them. This horrible operation was performed upon us, and the Iman applied the same balsam to us that is applied to children. We were all ready to die.

The Janissaries had scarce finished the feast with which we had supplied them, when the Russians came in their flat bottomed boats, and not a single Janissary escaped. The Russians showed no concern about the condition we were in. As there are French surgeons in every country, one of them who was a person of very great skill, took us under his care and cured us; and I shall remember as long as I live that when my wounds were pretty well healed, he made me amorous proposals. To be short, he told us all to cheer up, and assured us that the like misfortune had happened in several sieges; and that it was the law of war.

As soon as my companions were able to walk, they were obliged to go to Moscow. I fell to the lot of a Boyard, who made me his gardener, and gave me twenty lashes with his whip every day. But my lord having been broke on the wheel, within two years after, along with thirty more Boyards, on account of some quarrel at court, I availed myself of this event, and made my escape. After traversing over all Russia, I was a long time servant to an innkeeper at Riga, afterwards at Rostock, Wismar, Leipsic, Cassel, Utrecht, Leyden, the Hague, and Rotterdam. I grew old in misery and disgrace, having only one half of my back, but still remembering that I was a king's daughter. A hundred times have I had thoughts of killing myself; but still I was fond of life. This ridiculous weakness is perhaps one of our most melancholy foibles. For can anything be more stupid, than to be desirous of continually carrying a burden, which one has a good mind to throw down on the ground? to dread existence, and yet preserve it? in a word, to caress the serpent that devours us, till he has gnawed our very heart out?

In the countries through which it has been my fate to travel, and in the inns where I have been a servant, I have seen a prodigious number of people who looked upon their own existence as a curse; but I never knew of more than eight who voluntarily put an end to their misery, *viz.*, three negroes, four Englishmen, and a German professor named *Robeck*. My last service was with Don Issachar the Jew, who placed me near your person, my fair lady. I am resolved to share your fate; and I have been more affected with your misfortunes than with my own. I should never have spoken of my sufferings, if you had not vexed me a little, and if it had not been customary, on board a ship, to tell stories, by way of amusement. In short, Miss, I have a good deal of experience, and I have known the world. Divert yourself, and prevail upon each passenger to tell you his story; and if there is one found who has not frequently cursed his life, and has not as often said to himself, that he was the unhappiest of mortals, I will give you leave to throw me into the sea, head foremost.

CHAPTER XIII

How Candide Was Obliged to Part from the Fair Cunegonde and the Old Woman

THE BEAUTIFUL CUNEGONDE HAVING HEARD THE OLD WOMAN'S story, paid her all the civilities that were due to a person of her rank and merit. She approved of her proposal, and engaged all the passengers, one after another, to relate their adventures, and then both Candide and she confessed that the old woman was in the right. "It is a great pity," said Candide, "that the sage Pangloss was hanged, contrary to custom, for he would tell us most surprising things concerning the physical and moral evils which cover both land and sea; and I should be bold enough, with due respect, to propose some objections."

While each passenger was relating his story, the ship advanced in her voyage. They landed at Buenos Aires. Cunegonde, Capt. Candide, and the old woman, waited on the governor, Don Fernandes d'Ibaraa, y Figueora, y Mascarenes, y Lampourdos, y Souza. This nobleman was possessed of pride suitable to a person dignified with so many titles. He spoke to other people with so noble a disdain, turned up his nose, carried his head so high, raised his voice so intolerably, assumed so imperious all air, and affected so lofty a gait, that all those who saluted him were tempted to beat him. He was an excessive lover of the fair sex. Cunegonde appeared to him the prettiest woman he had ever seen. The first thing he did, was to ask whether she was not the Captain's wife? The manner in which he put the question alarmed Candide. He durst not say that she was his wife, because, in reality she was not; He durst not tell him that she was his sister, because she was not that either, and though this officious lie might have been of service to him, yet his soul was too refined to betray the truth. "Miss Cunegonde," said he, "intends me the honor of marrying me, and we beseech your Excellency to grace our nuptials with your presence."

Don Fernandes d'Ibaraa, y Figueora, y Mascarenes, y Lampourdos, y Souza, turning up his mustaches, forced a grim smile, and ordered Capt. Candide to go and review his company. Candide obeyed, and the Governor remained alone with Miss Cunegonde. He declared his passion, protested that he would marry her the next day in the face of the church, or otherwise, as it should be agreeable to a person of her charms. Cunegonde desired a quarter of an hour to consider the proposal, to consult with the old woman, and to make up her mind.

Said the old woman, to Cunegonde, "Miss, you can reckon up seventy-two descents in your family, and not one farthing in your pocket. It is now in your power to be the wife of the greatest lord in South America, who has very pretty whiskers; and what occasion have you to pique yourself upon inviolable fidelity? You have been ravished by the Bulgarians; a Jew and an inquisitor have been in your good graces. Misfortunes have no law on their side. I confess, that were I in your place, I should have no scruples to marry the governor, and make the fortune of Capt. Candide."

While the old woman was thus speaking, with all the prudence which age and experience dictated, they descried a small vessel entering the port, which had on board an alcald and alguazils. The occasion of their voyage was this.

The old woman had shrewdly guessed, that it was a cavalier with a big sleeve that stole the money and jewels from Cunegonde in the city of Badajoz, when she and Candide were making their escape. The man having offered to sell some of the diamonds to a jeweller, the latter recognized them as the inquisitor's. The cavalier, before he was hanged, confessed he had stolen them. He described the persons he had stolen them from, and told the route they had taken. The flight of Cunegonde and Candide being by this means discovered, they were traced to Cadiz, where a vessel was immediately sent in pursuit of them; and now the vessel was in the port of Buenos Aires. A report was spread, that an Alcald was going to land, and that he was in pursuit of the murderers of my lord the grand inquisitor. The old woman saw in a moment what was to be done. "You cannot run away," said she to Cunegonde, "and you have nothing to fear; it was not you that killed my lord; and besides, the governor, who is in love with you, will not suffer you to be ill treated. Therefore stay here." She then ran to Candide: "Fly," said she, "or in an hour you will be burnt alive." He had not a moment to lose; but how could he part from Cunegonde, and where could he fly to for shelter?

CHAPTER XIV

How Candide and Cacambo Were Received by the Clerics of Paraguay

CANDIDE HAD BROUGHT SUCH A VALET WITH HIM FROM CADIZ, AS one often meets with on the coasts of Spain, and in the colonies. He was a quarter-blooded Spaniard, born of a mongrel in Tucuman, and had been a singing-boy, a sexton, a sailor, a factor, a soldier, and a lackey. His name was *Cacambo*, and he had a strong love for his master, because his master was a very good sort of man. Having saddled the two Andalusian horses with all expedition; "Let us go, Master, let us follow the old woman's advice, let us set off, and run without looking behind us." Candide dropped some tears: "Oh, my dear Cunegonde," said he, "must I leave you just at the time when the governor was going to have us married! Cunegonde, what will become of you in this strange country?" "She will do as well as she can," said Cacambo; "women are never at a loss; God will provide for her; let us run." "Whither art thou carrying me?" said Candide; "where are we going? what shall I do without Cunegonde?" "By St. James of Compostella," said Cacambo, "you were going to fight against the clerics; now let us go and fight *for* them. I know the road perfectly well; I will conduct you to their kingdom; they will be charmed to have a captain that knows the Bulgarian exercise; you will make a prodigious fortune; though one cannot find his account in one world, he may in another. It is a great pleasure to see new sights and perform new exploits."

"Have you been in Paraguay?" said Candide.

"Yes, in truth, I have," said Cacambo. "I was usher to the college and am acquainted with the government of the good clerics as well as I am with the streets of Cadiz. It is an admirable sort of government. The kingdom is upwards of three hundred leagues in diameter, and divided into thirty provinces. The rulers there, are masters of everything, and the people have nothing. It is the masterpiece of reason and justice. For my part I see nothing so divine as the clerics who wage war here against the Kings of Spain and Portugal, and in Europe are their advisers, who in this country, kill Spaniards, and at Madrid, send them counsel. This transports me; let us therefore push forward; you are going to be the happiest of mortals. What pleasure will it be to those rulers when they know that a captain who understands the Bulgarian exercise comes to offer them his service!"

As soon as they reach the first barrier, Cacambo told the advanced guard, that a captain desired to speak with my lord the commandant. They went to inform the chief guard of it. A Paraguayan officer ran on foot to the commandant, to impart the news to him. Candide and Cacambo were at first disarmed, and their two Andalusian horses were seized. The two strangers were introduced between two files of musketeers; the commandant was at the further end, with a cap on his head, his gown tucked up, a sword by his side, and a staff in his hand. He made a signal, and straightaway four and twenty soldiers surrounded the newcomers. A serjeant told them they must wait; that the commandant could not speak to them; that the lord ruler does not permit any Spaniard to open his mouth but in his presence, or to stay above three hours in the province. "And where is the lord ruler," said Cacambo. "He is upon the parade," answered the serjeant: "and you cannot kiss his spurs in less than three hours." "But," said Cacambo, "my master, the Captain, who is ready to die for hunger as well as myself, is not a Spaniard, but a German; cannot we have something for breakfast, while we wait for his lordship."

The serjeant went to give an account of this discourse to the commandant. "God be praised," said the commandant; "since he is a German, I may speak with him; bring him into my arbor." Candide was immediately conducted into a green pavilion, decorated with a very handsome balustrade of green and gilt marble, with intertextures of vines, containing parrots, humming-birds, fly-birds, Guinea-hens, and all other sorts of rare birds. An excellent breakfast was provided in vessels of gold, and while the Paraguayans were eating Indian corn mush out of wooden dishes, in the open fields, exposed to the sultry heat of the sun, the commandant retired to his arbor.

He was a very handsome young man, with a full face, tolerably fair, fresh colored, his eyebrows were arched, his eyes full of fire, his ears red, his lips like vermillion; his hair was somewhat fierce, but of a fierceness which differed both from that of a Spaniard and Cleric. They now returned to Candide and Cacambo the arms, which had been taken from them, together with the two Andalusian horses; which Cacambo took the liberty to feed near the arbor, keeping his eye upon them, for fear of a surprise.

Candide immediately kissed the hem of the commandant's garment; after which, they both sat down to table. "You are a German, then?" said the Cleric to him, in that language. "Yes," said Candide. In pronouncing these words, they looked at each other with extreme surprise, which they were not able to account for. "And what part of Germany do you belong to?" said the Cleric. "To the lower part of Westphalia," said Candide; "I was born in the Castle of Thunder-ten-tronckh." "Heavens! is it possible!' cried the commandant. "What a miracle is this!" cried Candide. "Is it You?" said the commandant, "'Tis impossible!" said Candide. On this they both fell backwards; but getting up again, they embraced each other, and shed tears of joy. "What! is it you, you! the brother of the fair Cunegonde! you that was slain by the Bulgarians! you, the Baron's son! are you a ruler at Paraguay? I must confess, that this is a strange world indeed! Ah! Pangloss! Pangloss! how pleased you would now be, if you had not been hanged."

The commandant ordered the negro slaves, and the Paraguayans, that poured out the liquor in cups of rock crystal, to retire. He thanked God, a thousand times; folded Candide in his arms:

their faces being all the while bathed in tears. "You will be more astonished, more affected, more out of your wits," said Candide, "when I tell you that Miss Cunegonde, your sister, who you thought was dead is as well as I am." "Where?" "In your neighborhood; at the house of the governor of Buenos Aires; and I came here to fight against you." Every word they spoke in this long conversation, heaped surprise upon surprise. Their souls dwelt upon their tongues, listened in their ears, and sparkled in their eyes. As they were Germans, they made a long meal, (according to custom), waiting for the lord ruler, when the commandant thus addressed their dear Candide.

CHAPTER XV

How Candide Killed the Brother of His Dear Cunegonde

"I SHALL EVER HAVE PRESENT TO MY MEMORY," SAID THE BARON, "that horrible day, wherein I saw my father and mother killed, and my sister ravished. When the Bulgarians were gone, my sweet sister was no where to be found; and I, together with my father and mother, two maids, and three little lads that were murdered, were flung into a cart, in order to be buried in a chapel, which belonged to the clerics, about two leagues distant from our family-castle. A cleric sprinkled us with holy water, which being very salty, and some drops falling into my eyes, he could perceive my eye-balls move; on which he put his hand on my side, and felt my heart beat; I was taken care of, and, in about three weeks time, no one would have thought that anything had ailed me. You know very well my dear Candide, I was very handsome, but I grew more so; on which account, the superior of the house, conceived a very great affection for me, and some time after sent me to training. The superior was then looking out for a recruit of young men from Germany. For the rulers of Paraguay take as few Spanish as they can; but choose foreigners, because they think they can tyrannize over them as they please. I was therefore made choice of, as a proper person to go to work in this vineyard. I set sail in company with a Polander and a Tirolesian. On my arrival, I was honored with a lieutenancy. At present I am a colonel. We shall give the King of Spain's army a warm reception; I can assure you that they will be beaten. Providence has sent you hither to assist us. But is it true, that my dear sister Cunegonde is in our neighborhood, at the governor of Buenos Aires's house?" Candide swore that it was as true as the gospel. On this their tears gushed out afresh.

The Baron could not refrain from embracing Candide, whom he called his brother, and his protector. "Ah, perhaps," said he, "we two may enter the city in triumph, and recover my sister Cunegonde." "There is nothing I could wish for more," said Candide, "for I expected to be married to her, and I have some hopes I shall yet." "The insolence of the fellow!" replied the Baron. "Can you dare to think of marrying my sister, who can show seventy-two quarterings in her coat of arms? How dare you have the effrontery to speak to me thus!" Candide being quite thunderstruck at this, replied, "my revered father, all the quarterings in the world do not signify a farthing. I have delivered your sister from the hands of a Jew, and an inquisitor; she lies under a great many obligations to me, and is willing to marry me. Master Pangloss always told me that all men are equal. I am determined to marry her." "We will see whether you will, you villain!" said the cleric Baron of Thunder-ten-tronckh, at the same time giving him a blow on the face with the flat part of his sword. Candide drew his weapon immediately, and plunged it up to the hilt in the Baron's body; but drawing it out again, and looking upon it as it reeked, he cried out, "O God! I have killed my old master, my friend, my brother-in-law. I am one of the best-natured men in the world, yet I have killed three men."

Cacambo, who stood sentry at the door of the arbor, and who heard the noise, ran in. "We have nothing now to do but to sell our lives as dearly as we can," said his master to him; "and if they should force their way into the arbor, let us at least die with our arms in our hands."

Cacambo, who had been in circumstances of a similar nature, did not stand long to rack his brains for an expedient, but took the dress which the Baron wore, put it upon Candide, gave him the dead man's cap, and made him mount his horse. All this was done in the twinkling of an eye. "Let us gallop away, master," says he; "everybody will take you for some cleric that is going express, and we shall get to the frontiers before they can overtake us."

They fled like lightning, before these words were quite out of his mouth, crying out in Spanish, "Make way, make way for the Colonel."

CHAPTER XVI

What Passed Between Our Two Travellers and Two Girls, Two Monkeys, and the Savages Called Oreillons

CANDIDE AND HIS VALET HAD GOT BEYOND THE PASS, BEFORE ANY person in the camp got the least intimation of the death of the German. The provident Cacambo had taken care to fill his wallet with bread, chocolate, ham, and some bottles of wine. They pushed with their Andalusian horses into a strange country, where they could not discover any path or road. At last, a pleasant meadow, which was divided by a river, presented itself to their eyes. Our two travellers turned their horses out to graze, and Cacambo proposed to his master to eat a bit, at the same time setting him the example. "Do you think," said Candide, "that I can feast upon ham, when I have killed the Baron's son, and find myself under a necessity never to see Cunegonde again as long as I live? What signifies it to prolong my days in misery, since I must spend them far away from her, a prey to remorse and despair? and what will the Journal of Trevoux say of me?"

Having thus spoke, he refused to eat a morsel. The sun was now set, when our two wanderers, to their very great surprise, heard faint cries, which seemed to come from women. It was not easy to determine these cries; they rose immediately, with all the anxiety and apprehension to which people are subject in a strange place, and immediately discovered that the noise was made by two girls, who ran, unclothed, on the banks of the meadow, pursued by two large monkeys. Candide was moved with pity, and as he had learned to shoot, among the Bulgarians, and was so good a marksman that he could hit a nut in a bush without touching the leaves, he took up his Spanish fuzee, which was double-charged, and killed the two monkeys. "God be praised, my dear Cacambo," said he; "I have delivered the two poor girls from this great danger. If I have been guilty of a sin in killing the inquisitor, I have now made ample amends for it by saving the lives of two innocent girls. They may chance to prove a couple of ladies of rank; and who knows but this adventure may do us great service, in this country?"

He was going on at this rate, thinking that he had done a great feat, but how great was his surprise, when he saw the two girls, instead of rejoicing, embrace the monkeys with marks of the most tender affection! they bathed their bodies with tears, and filled the air with shrieks that testified the deepest distress. "I never expected to have seen such a sight as this," said he to Cacambo; who replied, "You have done a fine piece of work, indeed, Sir, you have killed the ladies' sweethearts." "Their sweethearts! is it possible? Surely you are in jest, Cacambo; who the deuce could believe you to be in earnest?" "My dear Sir," replied Cacambo, "you are always for making mountains of mole-hills; why should you think it incredible, that in some countries monkeys enjoy the favors of the ladies." "Ay," replied Candide, "now I recollect, Mr. Pangloss has told me, that there may be many an instance of this kind, and that these mixtures gave birth to the Egipans, Fauns, and Satyrs; that a great many of the ancients had seen them with their own eyes; but I always looked upon it as a mere romance." "You ought, at present, to see your mistake," said Cacambo, "and own that the doctor was in the right for once. And you may see what those people do, who have not received a particular education. All I am afraid of is, that these ladies will play us some spiteful trick."

These wise reflections induced Candide to quit the meadow, and take to a wood; where he and Cacambo supped together; and, after heartily cursing the Portuguese inquisitor, the governor of Buenos Aires, and the Baron, they fell asleep.

On waking, they found that they could not stir, for the Oreillons, the inhabitants of the country, whom the two lasses had informed of their adventure, had bound them in the nighttime, with cords made of the bark of a tree. They were surrounded by a body of fifty Oreillons, stark naked, armed with arrows, clubs, and hatchets made of flint. Some of them were making a great cauldron boil, others preparing spits, and all of them crying out, "He's a cleric, he's a cleric; we will make him pay sauce for it; we will pick his bones for him; let us eat the cleric, let us eat the cleric."

"You may remember I told you my dear master," cried Cacambo, in a lamentable tone, "that those two lasses would play us some spiteful trick."

Candide perceiving the cauldron and the spits, cried out, "O Lord! we are certainly going to be roasted or boiled. Ah! if Mr. Pangloss had seen nature without disguise, would he have said whatever is, is right? It may be so; but I must confess it is a sad thing to have lost Miss Cunegonde, and to be roasted or boiled for food by the Oreillons."

Cacambo, was never at a loss for an invention; "Never despair," said he to the disconsolate Candide. "I understand the jargon of these people a little, and am going to speak to them." "Don't fail," said Candide, "to represent to them the inhumanity of cooking men, and what an unchristian practice it is."

"Gentlemen," says Cacambo, "you fancy that you are going to feast on a cleric to-day; a very good dish, I make no doubt, nor is there anything more just than to serve one's enemies so. In effect, the law of nature teaches us to kill our fellow creatures, and it is a principle which is put in practice all over the globe. If we do not make use of the right of eating him, it is because we have plenty of victuals without it; but as you have not that advantage, it must certainly be better for you to eat your enemies, than to fling away the fruit of your victories a feast to crows and ravens. But, Gentlemen, I suppose you would not relish to eat your friends. You fancy you are going to spit or boil a cleric, but, believe me, I assure you, it is your defender, it is the enemy of your enemies, that you are preparing to treat thus. As to myself, I was born among you. The gentleman you see here is my master, and so far from being a cleric, he has just now killed a cleric, and he is only dressed in his spoils, which is the cause of your mistake. In order to confirm my assertion, let one of you take his gown off, carry it to the first pass of the government of the fathers, and inform himself whether my master has not killed a cleric officer. It is an affair that won't take up much time, and you may always have it in your power to eat us, if you catch me in a lie. But if I have told you the truth, and nothing but the truth, you are too well acquainted with the principles of natural right, morality, and law, not to show us some favor."

The Oreillons were so fully convinced of the reasonableness of this proposal, that they deputed two of their chiefs to go and inform themselves of the truth of what he had told them. The two deputies acquitted themselves of their charge like men of sense, and returned soon with a favorable account. The Oreillons then unbound the prisoners, showed them a thousand civilities, offered them women, gave them refreshments, and conducted them back again to the confines of their state, crying all the while, like madmen, "He is no cleric, he is no cleric."

Candide could not help admiring the subject of his deliverance. "What a people!" said he; "what men! what manners! If I had not had the good luck to run Miss Cunegonde's brother through the body, I should inevitably have been eaten up. But, after all, the dictates of pure nature are always best, since this people, instead of eating me, showed me a thousand civilities as soon as they knew that I was not a cleric."

CHAPTER XVII

The Arrival of Candide and His Man at the Country of Eldorado

When they had reached the frontiers of the Oreillons, "You see now," said Cacambo to Candide, "that this part of the world is not one pin better than the other. Take a fool's advice for once, and let us return to Europe as fast as ever we can." "How is that possible?" said Candide; "And pray what part of it would you have us go to? If I go to my own country, the Bulgarians and Abarians kill all they meet with there; if I return to Portugal, I am sure I shall be burnt alive; if we stay in this country, we run the hazard of being roasted every moment. And again, how can I think of leaving that part of the globe where Miss Cunegonde lives?"

"Why, then, let us take our course towards Cayenne," said Cacambo; "we shall meet with some Frenchmen there, for you know they are to be met with all over the globe; perhaps they will give us some relief, and God may have pity upon us."

It was no easy matter for them to go to Cayenne, as they did not know wherebouts it lay; besides, mountains, rivers, precipices, banditti, and savages, were difficulties they were sure to encounter in their journey. Their horses died with fatigue, and their provisions were soon consumed. After having lived a whole month on the wild fruits, they found themselves on the banks of a small river, which was bordered by cocoa trees, which both preserved their lives, and kept up their hopes.

Cacambo, who was on all occasions as good a counsellor as the old woman, said to Candide, "We can hold out no longer; we have walked enough already, and here's an empty canoe upon the shore, let's fill it with cocoa, then get on board, and let it drift with the stream. A river always runs to some inhabited place. If we don't meet with what we like, we are sure to meet with something new." "Why, what you say is very right, e'en let us go," said Candide, "and recommend ourselves to the care of Providence."

They rowed some leagues between the two banks, which were enamelled with flowers in some places, in others barren, in some parts level, and in others very steep. The river grew broader as they proceeded, and at last, lost itself in a vault of frightful rocks, which reached as high as the clouds. Our two travellers still had the courage to trust themselves to the stream. The river now growing narrower drove them along with such rapidity and noise, as filled them with the utmost horror. In about four and twenty hours, they got sight of daylight again, but their canoe was dashed in pieces against the breakers. They were obliged to crawl from one rock to another for a whole league; after which, they came in sight of a spacious plain, bounded with inaccessible mountains. The country was highly cultivated, both for pleasure and profit; the useful and the ornamental were most agreeably blended. The roads were covered, or, more properly speaking, were adorned, with carriages, whose figure and materials were very brilliant, they were full of men and women, of an extraordinary beauty, and were drawn with great swiftness, by large red sheep, which for fleetness, surpassed the finest horses of Andalusia, Tetuan, or Mequinez.

"This certainly," said Candide, "is a better country than Westphalia." He and Cacambo got on shore near the first village they came to. The very children of the village were dressed in gold brocades, all tattered, playing at quoits, at the entrance of the town. Our two travellers from the other world, amused themselves with looking at them. The quoits were made of large round pieces, yellow, red, and green, and cast a surprising light. Our travellers' hands itched prodigiously to be fingering some of them; for they were almost certain, that they were either gold, emeralds, or rubies; the least of which, would have been no small ornament to the throne of the Great Mogul. "To be sure," said Cacambo, "these must be the children of the king of the country, diverting themselves at quoits." The master of the village, coming at that instant to call them to school; "That's the preceptor to the royal family," cried Candide.

The little brats immediately quitted their play, leaving their quoits and other playthings behind them. Candide picked them up, ran to the schoolmaster, and presented them to him with a great deal of humility, acquainting him, by signs, that their Royal Highnesses had forgot their gold and jewels. The master of the village smiled, and flung them upon the ground; and having stared at Candide with some degree of surprise, walked off.

Our travellers did not fail immediately to pick up the gold, rubies, and emeralds. "Where have we got to now?" cried Candide. "The princes of the blood must certainly be well educated here, since they are taught to despise both gold and jewels." Cacambo was as much surprised as Candide. At length they drew near to the first house in the village, which was built like one of our European palaces. There was a vast crowd of people at the door, and still a greater within. They heard very good music, and their nostrils were saluted by a most refreshing smell from the kitchen.

Cacambo went up to the door, and heard them speaking the Peruvian language, which was his mother-tongue; for every one of my readers knows that Cacambo was born at Tucuman, a village where they make use of no other language. "I'll be your interpreter, master," cried Cacambo, in the greatest rapture, "this is a tavern, in with you, in with you."

Immediately, two waiters and two maids that belonged to the house, dressed in cloths of gold tissue, and having their hair tied back with ribbons, invited them to sit down to table with the landlord. They served up four soups, each garnished with two parroquets, a boiled vulture that weighed about two hundred pounds, two apes roasted, of an excellent taste, three hundred hummingbirds in one plate, and six hundred flybirds in another; together with exquisite ragouts, and the most delicious tarts, all in plates of a species of rock-crystal. After which, the lads and lasses served them with a great variety of liquors made from the sugar cane.

The guests were mostly tradesmen and carriers, all extremely polite, who asked some questions of Cacambo, with the greatest discretion and circumspection, and received satisfactory answers.

When the repast was ended, Cacambo and Candide thought to discharge their reckoning, by putting down two of the large pieces of gold which they had picked up. But the landlord and landlady burst into a loud fit of laughing, and could not restrain it for some time. Recovering themselves at last; "Gentlemen," says the landlord, "we can see pretty well that you are strangers; we are not much used to such guests here. Pardon us for laughing, when you offered us the stones of our highways in discharge of your reckoning. It is plain, you have got none of the money of this kingdom; but there is no occasion for it, in order to dine here. All the inns, which are established for the conveniency of trade, are maintained by the government. You have had but a sorry entertainment here, because this is but a poor village; but anywhere else, you will be sure to be received in a manner suitable to your merit."

Cacambo explained the host's speech to Candide, who heard it with as much astonishment and wonder as his friend Cacambo interpreted it. "What country can this be," said they to each other, "which is unknown to the rest of the world, and of so different a nature from ours? it is probably that country where everything really is for the best; for it is absolutely necessary that there should be one of that sort. And in spite of all Doctor Pangloss's arguments, I could not help thinking that things were very bad in Wesphalia."

CHAPTER XVIII

What They Saw in the Country of Eldorado

Cacambo could not conceal his curiosity from his landlord. "For my part," said the latter to him, "I am very ignorant, and I am well aware of it; but we have an old man here, who has retired from court, and is reckoned both the wisest and most communicative person in the kingdom." So saying, without any more ado, he conducted Cacambo to the old man's house. Candide acted now only the second personage, and followed his servant. They entered into a very plain house, for the door was nothing but silver, and the ceilings nothing but gold, but finished with so much taste, that the handsomest ceilings of Europe did not surpass them. The ante-chamber was indeed only covered with rubies and emeralds, but the order in which everything was arranged, made amends for this great simplicity.

The old gentleman received the two strangers on a sofa stuffed with the feathers of hummingbirds, and ordered them to be served with liquors in vessels of diamond; after which he satisfied their curiosity in the following manner.

"I am now in my hundred and seventy-second year, and I have heard my deceased father, who was groom to his Majesty, mention the surprising revolutions of Peru, of which he was an eyewitness. The kingdom we are in at present is the ancient country of the Incas, who left it very indiscreetly, in order to conquer one part of the world; instead of doing which, they themselves were all destroyed by the Spaniards.

"The princes of their family who remained in their native country were more wise; they made a law, by the unanimous consent of their whole nation, that none of our inhabitants should ever go out of our little kingdom; and it is owing to this that we have preserved both our innocence and our happiness. The Spaniards have had some confused idea of this country, and have called it *Eldorado*; and an Englishman, named Sir *Walter Raleigh*, has been on our coasts, above a hundred years ago; but as we are surrounded by inaccessible rocks and precipices, we have hitherto been sheltered from the rapacity of the European nations, who are inspired with an insensate rage for the stones and dirt of our land; to possess these, I verily believe they would not hesitate a moment to murder us all."

The conference between Candide and the old man was pretty long, and turned upon the form of government, the manners, the women, the public amusements, and the arts of Eldorado. At last, Candide, who had always a taste for Metaphysics, bid Cacambo ask if there was any religion in that country?

The old gentleman, reddening a little, "How is it possible," said he, "that you should question it? Do you take us for ungrateful wretches?" Cacambo then humbly asked him, what the religion of Eldorado was? This made the old gentleman redden again. "Can there be more religions than one?" said he; "we profess, I believe, the religion of the whole world; we worship the deity from evening to morning." "Do you worship one God?" said Cacambo, who still acted as interpreter in explaining Candide's doubts. "You may be sure we do," said the old man, "since it is evident there can be neither two, nor three, nor four. I must say, that the people of your world propose very odd questions." Candide was not yet wearied in interrogating the good old man; he wanted to know how they prayed to God in Eldorado. "We never pray at all," said the respectable sage; "we have nothing to ask of him; he has given us all we need, and we incessantly return him thanks."

Candide had a curiosity to see their priests, and bid Cacambo ask, where they were. This made the old gentleman smile. "My friends," said he, "we are all of us priests; the king, and the heads of each family, sing their songs of thanksgiving every morning, accompanied by five or six thousand musicians." "What!" said Cacambo, "have you no clerics to preach, to dispute, to tyrannize, to set people together by the ears, and to get those burnt who are not of the same opinions as themselves?" "We must be very great fools indeed if we had," said the old gentleman; "we are all of us of the same opinion, here, and we don't understand what you mean by clerics."

Candide was in an ecstasy during all this discourse, and said to himself, "This place is vastly different from Westphalia, and my lord the Baron's castle. If our friend Pangloss had seen Eldorado, he would never have maintained, that nothing upon earth could surpass the castle of Thunder-ten-tronckh. It is plain that everybody should travel."

After this long conversation was finished, the good old man ordered a coach and six sheep to be got ready, and twelve of his domestics to conduct the travellers to the court. "Excuse me," says he to them, "if my age deprives me of the honor of attending you. The king will receive you in a manner that you will not be displeased with, and you will, I doubt not, make allowance for the customs of the country, if you should meet with anything that you disapprove of."

Candide and Cacambo got into the coach, and the six sheep were so fleet, that in less than four hours they reached the King's palace, which was situated at one end of the metropolis. The gate was two hundred and twenty feet high, and one hundred broad; it is impossible to describe the materials it was composed of. But one may easily guess, that it must have prodigiously surpassed those stones, and the sand which we call gold and jewels.

Candide and Cacambo, on their alighting from the coach, were received by twenty maids of honor, of an exquisite beauty, who conducted them to the baths, and presented them with robes made of the down of hummingbirds; after which, the great officers and their ladies introduced them into his Majesty's apartment, between two rows of musicians, consisting of a thousand in each, according to the custom of the country.

When they approached the foot of the throne, Cacambo asked one of the great officers, in what manner they were to behave when they went to pay their respects to his Majesty; whether they were to fall down on their knees, or their bellies; whether they were to put their hands upon their heads or upon their backs; whether they were to lick up the dust of the room; and, in a word, what the ceremony was?" "The custom is," said the great officer, "to embrace the King, and kiss him on both cheeks." Candide and Cacambo accordingly clasped his Majesty round the neck, who received them in the most polite manner imaginable, and very genteelly invited them to sup with him.

In the interim, they showed them the city, the public edifices, that seemed almost to touch the clouds; the market places, embellished with a thousand columns; fountains of pure water, besides others of rose-water, and the liquors that are extracted from the sugar canes, which played continually in the squares, which were paved with a kind of precious stones, that diffused a fragrance like that of cloves or cinnamon. Candide asking them to show them their courts of justice, and their parliament house, they told him they had none, and that they were strangers to law-suits. He then inquired if they had any prisons, and was told they had not. What surprised him most, and gave him the greatest pleasure, was the palace of sciences, in which he saw a gallery two thousand paces in length, full of mathematical instruments and scientific apparatus.

After having spent the afternoon in going over about a thousandth part of the city, they were re-conducted to the palace. Candide seated himself at table with his Majesty, his valet Cacambo, and a great many ladies. Never was there a better entertainment; and never was more wit shown at table than what his Majesty displayed. Cacambo interpreted the King's repartees to Candide, and though they were translated, they appeared excellent repartees still; a thing which surprised Candide about as much as anything else.

They spent a whole month in this hospitable manner; Candide continually remarking to Cacambo, "I must say it again and again, my friend, that the castle where I was born, was nothing in comparison to the country where we are now; but yet Miss Cunegonde is not here, and without doubt, you have left a sweetheart behind you in Europe. If we stay where we are, we shall be looked upon only as other folks; whereas, if we return to our own world, only with twelve sheep loaded with pebbles of Eldorado, we shall be richer than all the kings put together; we shall have no need to be afraid of the inquisitors, and we may easily recover Miss Cunegonde."

This proposal was extremely agreeable to Cacambo; so fond are we of running about, of making a figure among our countrymen, of telling our exploits, and what we have seen in our travels, that these two really happy men resolved to be no longer so, and accordingly asked his Majesty's leave to depart.

"You are very foolish," said his Majesty to them. "I am not ignorant that my country is a small affair, but when one is well off it's best to keep so. I certainly have no right to detain strangers; it is a degree of tyranny inconsistent with our customs and laws; all men are free; you may depart when you please; but you cannot get away without the greatest difficulty. It is impossible to go against the current up the rapid river which runs under the rocks; your passage hither was a kind of miracle. The mountains which surround my kingdom are a thousand feet high, and as steep as a wall; they are at least ten leagues over, and their descent is a succession of precipices. However, since you seem determined to leave us, I will immediately give orders to the constructors of my machines, to make one to transport you comfortably. When they have conveyed you to the other side of the mountains, no one must attend you; because my subjects have made a vow never to pass beyond them, and they are too wise to break it. There is nothing else you can ask of me which shall not be granted." "We ask your Majesty," said Cacambo, very eagerly, "only a few sheep loaded with provisions, together with some of the common stones and dirt of your country."

The King laughed heartily; "I cannot," said he, "conceive what pleasure you Europeans find in our yellow clay; but you are welcome to take as much of it as you please, and much good may it do you."

He gave immediate orders to his engineers to construct a machine to hoist up and transport these two extraordinary persons out of his kingdom. Three thousand able mechanics set to work, and in a fortnight's time the machine was completed, which cost no more than twenty millions sterling of their currency.

Candide and Cacambo were both placed on the machine, together with two large red sheep bridled and saddled for them to ride on, when they were over the mountains, twenty sheep of burden, loaded with provisions, thirty with the greatest curiosities of the country, by way of present, and fifty with gold, precious stones, and diamonds. The King, after tenderly embracing the two vagabonds, took his leave of them.

It was a very fine spectacle to see them depart, and the ingenious manner in which they and the sheep were hoisted over the mountains. The contrivers of the machine took their leave of them, after having got them safe over, and now Candide had no other desire and no other aim, than to go to present his sheep to Miss Cunegonde. "We have now got enough," said he, "to pay for the ransom of Miss Cunegonde, no matter what price the governor of Buenos Aires puts upon her. Let us march towards Cayenne, there take shipping, and then we will determine what kingdom to make a purchase of."

CHAPTER XIX

What Happened to Them at Surinam, and How Candide Became Acquainted with Martin

The first day's journey of our two travellers was very agreeable, they being elated with the idea of finding themselves masters of more treasure than Asia, Europe, or Africa could scrape together. Candide was so transported, that he carved the name of Cunegonde upon almost every tree that he came to. The second day, two of their sheep sunk in a morass, and were lost, with all that they carried; two others died of fatigue a few days after; seven or eight died at once of want, in a desert; and some few days after, some others fell down a precipice. In short, after a march of one hundred days, their whole flock amounted to no more than two sheep.

"My friend," said Candide to Cacambo, "you see how perishable the riches of this world are; there is nothing durable, nothing to be depended on but virtue, and the happiness of once more seeing Miss Cunegonde." "I grant it," said Cacambo; "but we have still two sheep left, besides more treasure than ever the King of Spain was master of; and I see a town a good way off, that I take to be Surinam, belonging to the Dutch. We are at the end of our troubles, and at the beginning of our happiness."

As they drew nigh to the city, they saw a negro stretched on the ground, more than half naked, having only a pair of drawers of blue cloth; the poor fellow had lost his left leg and his right hand. "Good God!" said Candide to him, in Dutch, "what do you here, in this terrible condition?" "I am waiting for my master, Mynheer Vanderdendur, the great merchant," replied the negro. "And was it Mynheer Vanderdendur that used you in this manner?" said Candide. "Yes sir," said the negro, "it is the custom of the country. They give us a pair of linen drawers for our whole clothing twice a year. If we should chance to have one of our fingers caught in the mill, as we are working in the sugarhouses, they cut off our hand; if we offer to run away, they cut off one of our legs; and I have had the misfortune to be found guilty of both these offences. Such are the conditions on which you eat sugar in Europe! Yet when my mother sold me for ten crowns at Patagonia on the coast of Guinea, she said to me, My dear boy, bless our fetiches, adore them always, they will make you live happily. You have the honor to be a slave to our lords, the whites, and will by that means be in a way of making the fortunes both of your father and your mother. Alas! I do not know whether I have made their fortunes, but I am sure they have not made mine. The dogs, monkeys, and parrots, are a thousand times less wretched than we. The Dutch missionaries who converted me, told me every Sunday, that we all are sons of Adam, both blacks and whites. I am not a genealogist, myself; but if these preachers speak the truth, we are all cousins-german; and you must own, that it is a shocking thing to use one's relations in this barbarous manner."

"Ah! Pangloss," cried Candide, "you never dreamed of such an abominable piece of cruelty and villainy! there is an end of the matter; I see I must at last renounce your optimism." "What do you mean by optimism?" said Cacambo. "Why," said Candide, "it is the folly of maintaining that everything is right, when it is wrong." He then looked upon the negro with tears in his eyes, and entered Surinam weeping.

Their first business was to inquire whether there was any vessel in the harbor wherein they could hire a passage for Buenos Aires. The person they applied to was no other than a Spanish commander, who offered to make an honorable bargain with them. He appointed to meet them at an inn, whither Candide and the faithful Cacambo went to wait for him with their two sheep.

Candide, whose heart was always on his lips, told the Spaniard his adventures, and confessed that he was determined to run away with Miss Cunegonde. "I shall take care how I carry you to Buenos Aires, if that is the case," said the captain; "for I should be hanged, and so would you. The fair Cunegonde is my Lord's favorite mistress."

This was a thunder-clap to Candide; he wept a long time, but at last, drawing Cacambo aside, "I will tell you, my dear friend," said he, "what I would have you do. We have each of us about five or six millions of diamonds in our pocket; and as you are smarter at a bargain than I am, go you and fetch Miss Cunegonde from Buenos Aires. If the governor should make any objection, give him a million diamonds; if that does not succeed, give him two millions. As you did not murder the inquisitor, they will have no complaint against you; in the meantime, I will fit out another vessel, and go and wait for you at Venice; that is a safe place, and I need not be afraid there of Bulgarians, Abares, Jews, or Inquisitors." Cacambo applauded this sage resolution. He was, indeed, under great concern at leaving so good a master, who used him like a familiar friend; but the pleasure of being serviceable to him soon got the better of the sorrow he felt in parting with him.

They took leave of each other with tears; Candide recommending to him at the same time not to forget their good old woman. The same day Cacambo set sail. This Cacambo was a very honest fellow.

Candide stayed some time at Surinam, waiting for another vessel to carry him and the two remaining sheep to Italy. He hired servants, and purchased everything necessary for so long a voyage; at last, Mynheer Vanderdendur, the master of a large vessel, came and offered his service. "What will you charge?" said he to the Dutchman, "for carrying me, my servants, goods, and the two sheep you see here, directly to Venice?" The master of the vessel asked ten thousand piastres; Candide made no objection.

"Oh, oh," said the crafty Vanderdendur to himself, after he had left him, "if this stranger can give ten thousand piastres, without any words about it, he must be immensely rich." Returning a few minutes after, he let him know, that he could not go for less than twenty thousand. "Well, you shall have twenty thousand then," said Candide.

"Odso," said the captain with a low voice, "this man makes no more of twenty thousand piastres than he did of ten!" He then returned a second time, and said that he could not carry him to Venice for less than thirty thousand piastres. "You shall have thirty thousand then," replied Candide.

"Oh, oh," said the Dutch trader again to himself, "this man makes nothing of thirty thousand piastres; no doubt but the two sheep are loaded with immense treasures; let us stand out no longer; let us, however, finger the thirty thousand piastres first, and then we shall see."

Candide sold two small diamonds, the least of which was worth more than what the captain had asked. He advanced him the money. The two sheep were put aboard the vessel. Candide followed in a small wherry, intending to join the vessel in the road. But the captain improved his opportunity, unfurled sails, and unmoored. The wind being favorable, Candide, distracted and out of his wits, soon lost sight of him. "Ah!" cried he, "this is a trick worthy of the old world." He returned on shore, overwhelmed with sorrow; for he had lost more than would have made the fortunes of twenty princes.

He ran immediately to the Dutch judge, and as he hardly knew what he was about, knocked very loud at the door; he went in, told his case, and raised his voice a little higher than became him. The judge began by making him pay ten thousand piastres for the noise he had made; after which he heard him very patiently, and promised to examine into the affair, as soon as ever the trader should return; at the same time, making him pay ten thousand piastres more for the expense of hearing his case.

This proceeding made Candide stark mad. He had indeed experienced misfortunes a thousand times more affecting, but the coolness of the judge, and the knavish trick of the master of the vessel who had robbed him, fired his spirits, and plunged him into a profound melancholy. The villainy of mankind presented itself to his mind in all its deformity, and he dwelt upon nothing but the most dismal ideas. At last, a French vessel being ready to sail for Bordeaux, as he had no sheep loaded with diamonds to carry with him, he paid the common price as a cabin passenger, and ordered the crier to give notice all over the city, that he would pay the passage and board of any honest man that would go the voyage with him, and give him two thousand piastres besides, on condition that he would make it appear, that he was the most disgusted with his condition, and the most wretched person in that province.

A vast multitude of candidates presented themselves, enough to have manned a fleet. Candide selected twenty from among them, who seemed to have the best pretensions, and to be the most sociable. But as every one of them thought the preference due to himself, he invited them all to his inn, and gave them a supper, on condition that each one of them should take an oath, that he would relate his adventures faithfully, promising to choose that person who seemed to be the greatest object of pity, and had the greatest reason to be dissatisfied with his lot, and to give a small present to the rest, as a recompense for their trouble.

The assembly continued till four o'clock the next morning. As Candide was employed in hearing their adventures, he could not help recollecting what the old woman had told him during their voyage to Buenos Aires, and the bet she had made, that there was not a single person in the ship, that had not experienced some terrible misfortune. He thought of Pangloss at every adventure that was related. "That Pangloss," said he, "would be hard put to it to defend his system now. I wish he was but here. Indeed, if everything is ordered for the best, it must be at Eldorado, but nowhere else on earth." At last, he decided in favor of a poor scholar, who had wrote ten years for the booksellers at Amsterdam. For he thought there could not be a more disagreeable employment in the world.

This scholar, though in other respects a good sort of a man, had been robbed by his wife, beat by his son, abandoned by his daughter, who got a Portuguese to run away with her; had been stripped of a small employment, which was all he had to subsist on, and was persecuted by the clerics at Surinam, because they took him for a Socinian.

It must indeed be confessed, that most of the other candidates were as unhappy as he; but he met with a preference, because Candide thought that a scholar was best calculated to amuse him during the voyage. All his competitors thought that Candide did them a great piece of injustice; but he appeased them by giving each of them a hundred piastres.

CHAPTER XX

What Happened to Candide and Martin at Sea

THE OLD SCHOLAR, WHO WAS NAMED *MARTIN*, EMBARKED FOR BORDEAUX along with Candide. They had both of them seen and suffered a great deal; and if the vessel had been going to sail from Surinam to Japan, by the way of the Cape of Good Hope, they would have found enough wherewith to entertain themselves on the subject of physical and moral evil, during the whole voyage.

Candide, however, had one great advantage over Martin, which was, that he still hoped to see Miss Cunegonde again; but as for Martin, he had nothing to hope for; to which we may add, that Candide had both gold and diamonds; and though he had lost a hundred large red sheep, loaded with the greatest treasure that the earth could produce, through the knavery of the Dutch captain was always uppermost in his thoughts, yet when he reflected upon what he had still left in his pockets, and when he talked about Cunegonde, especially toward the latter end of a hearty meal, he inclined to Pangloss's hypothesis.

"But you, Mr. Martin," said he to the scholar, "what is your opinion? what is your notion of physical and moral evil?" "Sir," replied Martin, "the clerics have accused me of being a Socinian; but the truth is I am a Manichean."

"You are in jest, sure," said Candide; "there are no longer any Manicheans in the world!" "I am one, though," said Martin; "I cannot well account for it, but yet I am not able to think otherwise."

"The devil must be in you, then," said Candide. "He concerns himself so much in the affairs of this world," said Martin, "that he may possibly be in me as well as anywhere else; but I must confess that when I cast my eyes over this globe, or rather over this globule, I cannot help thinking that God has abandoned it to some malignant being: I always except Eldorado. I never met with a city that did not wish the destruction of its neighbor city, nor one family that did not desire to exterminate another family. All over the world, the poor curse the rich, to whom they are obliged to cringe; and the rich treat the poor like so many sheep, whose wool and flesh is sold to the highest bidder. A million assassins, formed into regiments, scour Europe from one extremity to another, committing murder and rapine systematically and according to discipline, for their bread, because they cannot find a more honest or honorable profession; and in those cities which seem to enjoy the blessings of peace, and where the arts are cultivated, mankind are devoured with greater envy, care, and disquietude, than a city meets with when it is besieged. Private torments are still more insupportable than public calamities. In a word, I have seen and experienced so much that I have become a Manichean."

"There's some good in the world, for all that," replied Candide. "That may be," said Martin, "but I do not know where to find it."

In the midst of this dispute, they heard the report of cannon. The noise increasing every moment, each person took out his spyglass, and soon clearly discovered two vessels about three miles distant, engaged in battle. The wind brought the combatants so near the French vessel, that they had the pleasure of seeing the fight very clearly. At length one of the vessels gave the other a broadside between wind and water, which sunk it to the bottom. Candide and Martin plainly perceived about a hundred men on the deck of the ship which was sinking, lifting up their hands towards heaven, and making the most dismal lamentations; and in an instant they were all swallowed up by the sea.

"Well," said Martin, "see how mankind treat one another." "It is true," said Candide, "there's something diabolical in this affair." As he was saying this, he perceived something red and glittering swimming near his ship. They immediately sent the longboat to see what it could be, when it proved to be one of those red sheep. Candide felt more of joy at the recovery of this sheep, than he had of trouble at the loss of a hundred such, loaded with the large diamonds of Eldorado.

The French captain soon found that the captain of the conquering vessel was a Spaniard, and that the commander of the vessel which was sunk was a Dutch pirate, and the very same who had robbed Candide. The immense riches which the villain had amassed were buried in the sea along with him, and there was only a single sheep saved.

"You see," said Candide to Martin, "that wickedness sometimes meets with condign punishment; that rascal, the Dutch commander, has met with the fate he merited." "Yes," said Martin; "but why should the passengers on board of his ship also perish together with him? God indeed has punished the villain, but he has permitted the devil to drown the rest."

In the meantime, the Frenchman and the Spaniard continued their course, and Candide pursued his debates with Martin. They disputed fifteen days without intermission; and, at the end of the fifteen days, both were as far from being convinced as when they began. But they chatted, intercommunicated their ideas, and amused each other reciprocally. Candide caressing his sheep, "Since I have found you," said he, "I have some hopes of recovering Cunegonde."

CHAPTER XXI

Candide and Martin Draw Near to the Coast of France and Continue to Discuss

At length they descried the coast of France. "Have you ever been in France, Mr. Martin?" said Candide. "Yes," said Martin, "I have travelled over several of its provinces. In some, half the inhabitants are mere fools; in others, they are too cunning; in others, either very polite and good natured, or very brutish; in others, they affect to be wits; and in all of them the chief occupation is love, the next lying, and the third to talk nonsense." "But, Mr. Martin, have you ever been in Paris?" "Yes, I have; the people are just the same there; it is a mere chaos; a crowd in which everyone is in search after pleasure, but no one finds it, as far as I have been able to discover. I spent a few days there on my arrival, and I was robbed of all I had, by some sharpers, at the fair of St. Germain. Nay, I myself was taken up for a robber, and was eight days in prison; after which I turned corrector of the press, to get a small matter to carry me on foot to Holland. I know the whole tribe of scribblers, with malcontents and fanatics. They say the people are very polite in that city; I wish I could believe them."

"For my part, I have no curiosity to see France," said Candide; "you may easily fancy that when a person has once spent a month at Eldorado, he is very indifferent whether he sees anything else on earth, except Miss Cunegonde. I am going to wait for her at Venice; we will go through France, in our way towards Italy. Won't you bear me company?" "With all my heart," said Martin; "they say that Venice is not fit for any but the noble Venetians; but, for all that, they receive strangers very well, provided they have a good deal of money. I have none; you have; therefore, I'll follow you all the world over." "Now I think of it," said Candide, "do you imagine that the earth was originally nothing but water, as is asserted in the great book belonging to the Captain?" "I don't believe a word of it," said Martin, "no more than I do of all the reveries that have been published for some time." "But for what end was the world created, then," said Candide. "To make people mad," replied Martin. "Were not you greatly surprised," continued Candide, at the story I told you of the passion which the two girls in the country of the Oreillons had for those two apes?" "Not at all," said Martin; "I see nothing strange in that passion; for I have seen so many strange things already, that I can look upon nothing as extraordinary." "Do you believe," said Candide, "that mankind have always been cutting one another's throats; that they were always liars, knaves, treacherous and ungrateful; always thieves, sharpers, highwaymen, lazy, envious and gluttons; always drunkards, misers, ambitious and blood-thirsty; always backbiters, debauchees, fanatics, hypocrites and fools?" "Do you not believe," said Martin, "that hawks have always preyed upon pigeons, when they could light upon them?" "Certainly," said Candide. "Well, then," said Martin, "if the hawks have always had the same nature, what reason can you give why mankind should have changed theirs?" "Oh!" said Candide, "there is a great deal of difference, because free-will . . ."

In the midst of this dispute, they arrived at Bordeaux.

CHAPTER XXII

What Happened in France to Candide and Martin

CANDIDE STAYED NO LONGER AT BORDEAUX THAN TILL HE COULD dispose of some of the pebbles of Eldorado, and furnish himself with a post-chaise large enough to hold two persons; for he could not part with his philosopher Martin. He was indeed very sorry to part with his sheep, which he left at the Academy of Sciences at Bourdeaux, which proposed for the subject of this year's prize, the reason why this sheep's wool was red; and the prize was adjudged to a learned man in the North, who demonstrated, by A *plus* B *minus* C divided by Z, that the sheep must be red, and die of the rot.

In the meantime, all the travellers whom Candide met in the inns on the road, telling him they were going to Paris, this general eagerness to see the capital inspired him, at length, with the same desire, as it was not much out of the way in his journey towards Venice.

He entered Paris by the suburb of St. Marçeau, and fancied himself to be in the dirtiest village in Westphalia.

Candide had scarce got to his inn, when he was seized by a slight indisposition, caused by his fatigues. As he had a very large diamond on his finger, and the people had taken notice of a pretty heavy box among his baggage, in a moment's time he had no less than two physicians to attend him, who did not wait to be sent for; a few intimate friends, that never left him, sat up with him together with a couple of female friends that took care to have his broths warmed. "I remember," said Martin, "that when I was sick at Paris, in my first journey, I was very poor, and could meet neither with friends, nurses, nor physicians; but I recovered."

Meanwhile, by medicines and bleedings, Candide's disorder grew more serious, and the clerk of the town came, with great modesty to ask a bill for the other world, payable to the bearer. Candide refused to accord it; the nurses assured him that it was a new fashion. Candide replied, that he was resolved not to follow the fashion. Martin was going to throw the clerk out of the window. The clerk swore that Candide should not be buried. Martin swore he would bury the clerk, if he continued to be troublesome. The quarrel grew high, and Martin took the clerk by the shoulders, and pushed him out of doors. This occasioned a great deal of scandal, and an action was commenced against him.

Candide recovered, and while he was convalescent, had the best company to sup with him. They gamed high and Candide was very much surprised that he never could throw an ace; but Martin was not surprised at all.

Among those who did him the honors of the city, was a little cleric of Périgord, one of those people that are always busy, always alert, always ready to do one service, forward, fawning, and accommodating themselves to everyone's humor; who watch for strangers on their journey, tell them the scandalous history of the town, and offer them help at all prices. This man took Candide and Martin to the playhouse, where a new tragedy was to be acted. Candide found himself seated near the critics, but this did not prevent him from weeping at some scenes that were well acted. One of these critics, who stood at his elbow, said to him, in the midst of one of the acts, "You were in the wrong to shed tears; that's a shocking actress, the actor who plays with her is worse than she is, and the piece is still worse than the actors. The author does not understand a single word of Arabic, and yet the scene lies in Arabia; but besides, he is a man who does not believe that our ideas are innate. I'll bring you twenty pamphlets against him to-morrow."

"Pray sir," said Candide, to the cleric, "how many theatrical pieces have you in France?" "Five or six thousand," replied the other. "Indeed! that is a great many," said Candide; "but how many good ones are there among them?" "Some fifteen or sixteen," was the reply. "Oh, that is a great many," said Martin.

Candide was greatly taken with an actress who played Queen Elizabeth in a dull kind of tragedy, that was occasionally put on the stage. "That actress," said he to Martin, "pleases me greatly. She has some sort of resemblance to Miss Cunegonde. I should be very glad to pay my respects to her." The cleric of Périgord offered his services to introduce him to her at her own house. Candide, who was brought up in Germany, desired to be informed as to the ceremony used on these occasions, and how a queen of England was treated in France. "There is a distinction to be observed in these matters," said the cleric. "In the country towns, we take them to a tavern; here, in Paris, they are treated with great respect during their lifetime, provided they are handsome; and when they die, we throw their bodies on a dunghill." "How!" said Candide, "throw a queen's body on a dunghill?" "The gentleman is quite correct," said Martin; "he tells you nothing but the truth. I happened to be in Paris when Miss Mevina made her exit, as they say, from this world to the other. She was refused what they here call the rights of sepulture: that is, to say, she was denied the privilege of rotting in a church-yard with all the beggars in the parish. They buried her at the corner of Burgundy Street, which most certainly would have shocked her extremely, for she was very high spirited." "This was a very unfeeling act," said Candide. "What would you do?" said Martin. "It is the way of these people. Figure to yourself all the contradictions, and all the absurdities possible, and you will find them in the church, in the government, in the tribunals, and in the theatres, of this droll nation." "Is it true that the Parisians are always laughing?" said Candide. "Yes," said the cleric, "but it is with hearts full of anger. They complain amidst bursts of laughter; they even commit the most detestable actions, laughing all the while."

"Who," said Candide, "was that ill-mannered hog, who spoke so disparagingly of the scene in the play that made me weep, and of the actors who gave me so much pleasure?" "It is a miserable creature," replied the cleric, "who gets his living by running down all the new plays and all the new books. He hates those who meet with success, as eunuchs hate all who enjoy themselves. He is one of those literary serpents who nourish themselves on venom. He is a pamphleteer." "What do you call a pamphleteer?" said Candide. "It is," said the cleric, "a maker of pamphlets; a Freron."

Thus Candide, Martin, and the Périgordin conversed together, on the stairway, whilst seeing the spectators go out of the theatre. "Although I am very anxious to see Miss Cunegonde, I would like to sup with Mademoiselle Clairon, she appears so amiable," said Candide.

The cleric was not the man to approach Mademoiselle Clairon, who received only the best company. "She is engaged, this evening," said he; "but permit me the honor to introduce you to a lady of quality, who will make you as well acquainted with Paris, as though you had lived there four years."

Candide, who was naturally curious, allowed himself to be taken to the house of the lady, situated in the faubourg Saint Honoré; the company was playing at faro; twelve melancholy looking punters held each in their hands, a small pack of cards, with the corners turned down, as if to register their losses. Profound silence reigned. The faces of all the punters were very pale, he who held the bank was the very picture of anxiety, and the lady of the house, seated near this pitiless man, observed with the eyes of a lynx, every word, every *sept-et-le-va* with which each player of the company bent the corners of his cards; she made them straighten them out again; and was very strict in that respect, yet very polite, for fear of losing their custom. The lady assumed the title of Marchioness of Parolignac. Her daughter, about fifteen years of age, was one of the punters, and notified her mother by a wink of her eye, of the little tricks the poor people they were victimizing resorted to in trying to repair their losses.

Candide and Martin enter. No one rises, no one salutes them, nobody even looks at them; all are intensely occupied with their cards. "Madame the Baroness of Thunder-ten-tronckh was more polite," thought Candide.

Meanwhile, the cleric whispered in the ear of the marchioness, who, partly rising, honored Candide with a gracious smile, and Martin with a majestic nod. She ordered a seat and a hand of cards to be given to Candide, who lost fifty thousand francs in two deals. After which, they supped very merrily, and all the company were astonished that Candide was not in the least cast down by his losses. The waiters came to the conclusion among themselves, that he must be some English lord.

The supper was, like most suppers at Paris, begun in silence; afterwards, there was a noise of words that no one could distinguish. Then came insipid jokes, false news, and bad arguments; a little politics, and a great deal of scandal. They even conversed about new books. "Have you seen the romance of Mr. Gauchet, professor of philosophy?" said the cleric of Périgord. "Yes," replied one of the company, "but I couldn't finish reading it. We have a crowd of impertinent writers, but all of them together don't come up to the impertinence of Gauchet, professor of philosophy. I am so disgusted with this immensity of detestable books with which we are inundated, that I have taken to playing faro."

"And the Miscellanies of Troublet, what do you think of them?" said the cleric. "Ah!" said Madame de Parolignac; "the tiresome creature! How curiously he tells you what all the world knows. How weightily he discusses what is not worth being ever so lightly remarked. How he appropriates the genius of others without having the least genius himself. How he spoils what he steals; how he disgusts me; but he will disgust me no more; it is enough to have read a few pages.

There was at table a man of learning and taste, who inclined to what the marchioness had said. The conversation turning on tragedies, the lady asked how it happened that there were tragedies which were sometimes played, that nobody cared to read. The man of taste explained how a play could be somewhat interesting, yet have scarcely any merit. He proved, in a few words, that "it is not enough to introduce one or two of those scenes which are found in all the romances, and which always seduce the spectators. It is necessary to be new without being fickle, often sublime, and always natural; to understand the human heart, and make it speak; to be a good poet, without letting any character in the play appear like one; to be perfectly acquainted with language, to speak it with purity and continuous harmony, and never sacrifice sense to rhyme. Whoever," added he, "does not observe all these rules, may write one or two tragedies that will be applauded at the theatre, but he will never rank among good writers. There are very few good tragedies. Some are idyls in dialogue, well written and well rhymed; others are political reasonings which put us to sleep, or amplifications which repel us; others are dreams of demoniacs in barbarous style, desultory talk, long apostrophes to the gods because the author does not understand how to talk to men, false maxims and bombast."

Candide listened to all this with attention, and conceived a high opinion of the discourser; and as the marchioness had taken care to place him at her side, he took the liberty of asking, in a whisper, who this man was, who spoke so well. "It is a scholar," said the lady, "who never puntes, and whom the cleric sometimes brings along with him to supper. He is perfectly acquainted with tragedies and books, he has written a hissed tragedy, and a book which he dedicated to me; but the only copy that has ever seen the outside of the publisher's store, is the one he presented to me." "The great man!" said Candide, "he is another Pangloss."

Then, turning to him, he said: "Sir, you believe, no doubt, that all is for the best in the physical and moral world, and that nothing can be otherwise?" "Me," replied the scholar, "I don't think anything of the kind. I find that all goes contrary with us, that no one knows what is his rank, or what is his employment, or what he does, or what he ought to do; and except entertainments which are very gay, and over which there appears to be considerable union, all the rest of the time passes in impertinent quarrels, Jansenists against Molinists, members of parliament against dignitaries of the church, men of letters against men of letters, courtesans against courtesans, financiers against the people, wives against husbands, relations against relations; it is a continual warfare."

"I have seen the worst," replied Candide, "but a very great philosopher, who had the misfortune to be hanged, has taught me that all this is wonderfully well; a mere shadow on a very fine picture." "Your philosopher who has been hanged made a great fool of himself," said Martin; "your shadows are horrible blemishes." "It is men who make the blemishes," said Candide, "and they can't help it." "Then it is not their fault," said Martin. Most of the punters, who understood nothing of this language, employed their time in drinking. Martin kept on reasoning with the scholar, and Candide related a part of his adventures to the lady of the house.

After supper, the marchioness conducted Candide into her private room, and seated him on a sofa. "Ah, well, you love Miss Cunegonde, of Thunder-ten-tronckh, to distraction." "Yes, Madam," said Candide. To this the marchioness replied with a tender smile, "you answer me just like a young Westphalian; a Frenchman would have said:—"It is true that I did love Mademoiselle Cunegonde, but having seen you, Madam, I fear I shall never love her any more." "Well, Madam," said Candide, "I will answer thus if you wish." "Your passion for her," said the marchioness, "commenced in picking up her handkerchief; will you please to pick up my garter?" "With all my heart," said Candide, and he picked it up. "Now I want you to tie it on," said the lady; and Candide tied it on. "Look you," said the lady, "you are a stranger; I sometimes make my Parisian lovers languish a fortnight, but I surrender to you the first night, *parce qu'il faut faire les honneurs de son pays* to a young man from Westphalia. The lady perceiving two enormous diamonds worn by her young stranger, praised them so much that they immediately passed from the fingers of Candide to those of the marchioness.

Candide, in returning with the cleric of Périgord, expressed remorse for having been guilty of infidelity towards Miss Cunegonde; the cleric consoled him; he had only a small part of the fifty thousand francs which Candide lost at play, and of the value of the two brilliants, half given, half extorted. His design was to profit as much as he could from the advantages Candide's acquaintanceship might procure him. He talked continually of Cunegonde, and Candide assured him that he would ask pardon of this beauty when he should meet her at Venice.

The cleric redoubled his politeness and attentions, and took a very tender interest in all Candide said, in all he did, and in all he wished to do.

"You have then, sir," said he, "a *rendezvous* at Venice?" "Yes, Mr. Cleric," said Candide, "I must certainly go there, to find Miss Cunegonde." Then, led away by the pleasure of speaking of one he so loved, he related, as was his custom, a part of his adventures with this illustrious Westphalian.

"I fancy," said the cleric, "that Miss Cunegonde is a lady of very great accomplishments, and that she writes charming letters?" "I never received any letters from her," said Candide, "for, being driven out of the castle on account of my passion for her, I could not write to her; soon after, I heard she was dead; afterwards, I found her, and lost her; and I have now sent an express to her about two thousand five hundred leagues from hence, and wait for an answer."

The cleric heard him with great attention, and appeared to be a little thoughtful. He soon took leave of the two strangers, after a most affectionate embrace. The next day, as soon as Candide awoke, he received a letter couched in the following terms:

"My dearest love, I have been ill these eight days in this town, and have learned that you are here. I would fly to your arms, if I were able to stir. I knew of your passage to Bordeaux, where I have left the faithful Cacambo and the old woman, who are to follow me very soon. The governor of Buenos Aires has taken all from me, but your heart is still left me. Come; your presence will restore me to life, unless it kills me with pleasure."

This charming and unexpected letter, transported Candide with inexpressible joy, whilst the sickness of his dear Cunegonde overwhelmed him with sorrow. Distracted between these two passions, he took his gold and diamonds, and got somebody to conduct him and Martin to the house where Miss Cunegonde was lodged.

On his entrance, he trembled in every limb, his heart beat quick, and his voice was choked up with sighs; he asked them to bring a light, and was going to open the curtains of the bed. "Take care, sir," said the nurse, "she can't bear light, it would kill her"; and immediately she drew the curtains close again. "My dear Cunegonde," said Candide, weeping, "how do you find yourself? though you can't see me, you may speak to me, at least." "She cannot speak," said the maid. The sick lady then put a plump little hand out of the bed, which Candide for some time bathed with his tears, and afterwards filled with diamonds, leaving a bag full of gold upon the easy chair.

In the midst of his transports, a lifeguardman came in, followed by the Périgordin cleric and a file of soldiers. "There," said he, "are the two suspected foreigners." He caused them to be immediately seized, and ordered his men to drag them to prison. "It is not thus they treat travellers at Eldorado," said Candide. "I am more a Manichean than ever," said Martin. "But pray, sir, where are you going to carry us," said Candide. "To a hole in the lowest dungeon," said the lifeguardman.

Martin having recovered his usual coolness, saw at once that the lass who pretended to be Cunegonde was a cheat; that the Périgordin cleric was an impostor, who had taken advantage of Candide's simplicity; and that the lifeguardman was another sharper, whom they might easily get clear of.

Rather than expose himself before a court of justice, Candide, by his counsellor's advice, and besides, being very impatient to see the real Cunegonde, offered the lifeguardman three small diamonds, worth about 3,000 pistoles each. "Ah, sir," said the man with the ivory baton, "though you had committed all the crimes that can be imagined, this would make me think you the most honest gentleman in the world! Three diamonds! worth 3,000 pistoles apiece! Sir, instead of putting you in a dungeon, I would lose my life for you; all strangers are arrested here, but let me alone for that; I have a brother at Dieppe in Normandy; I'll conduct you thither, and if you have any diamonds to give him, he will take as good care of you as I would myself."

"And why do they put all strangers under arrest?" said Candide. The cleric of Périgord then put in his word: "Because," said he, "a knave of Atrebatia listened to some foolish stories, which made him commit a parricide, not like that in May, 1610, but like that in December, 1594; and just like those that a great many other knaves have been guilty of, in other months and other years, after listening to foolish stories."

The lifeguardman then gave him a more particular account of their crimes. "Oh! the monsters," cried Candide; "are there then such terrible crimes among people who dance and sing? Can I not immediately get out of this country, where monkeys provoke tigers? I have seen bears in my own country, but I never met with men except at Eldorado. In the name of God, Mr. Officer, conduct me to Venice, where I am to wait for Miss Cunegonde." "I can conduct you nowhere except to Lower Normandy," said the mock officer. Immediately he ordered his irons to be struck off, said he was under a mistake, discharged his men, conducted Candide and Martin to Dieppe, and left them in the hands of his brother.

There was then a small Holland trader in the harbor. The Norman, by means of three more diamonds, became the most serviceable man in the world, put Candide and his attendants safe on board the vessel, which was ready to sail for Portsmouth, in England.

This was not the way to Venice; but Candide thought he had escaped from hell, and resolved to resume his voyage towards Venice the first opportunity that offered.

CHAPTER XXIII

Candide and Martin Go to the English Coast, and What They Saw There

"AH! PANGLOSS! PANGLOSS! AH! MARTIN! MARTIN! AH! MY DEAR Cunegonde! what a world is this!" said Candide on board the Dutch ship. "A very foolish and abominable one indeed," replied Martin. "You are acquainted with England, then," said Candide; "are they as great fools there as in France?" "They have a different kind of folly," said Martin. "You know that these two nations are at war about a few acres of snow in Canada, and that they have spent a great deal more upon this war than all Canada is worth. To tell you precisely whether there are more people who ought to be confined in a madhouse in one country than in the other, is more than my weak capacity is able to perform. I only know in general that the people we are going to see are very melancholic."

As they were talking in this manner, they arrived at Portsmouth. The shore was covered with a multitude of people, who were looking very attentively at a pretty stout man who was kneeling, with his eyes bandaged, on the deck of a ship of war; four soldiers, that were placed opposite to him, shot three balls apiece through his head, with the greatest coolness imaginable, and the whole assembly went away very well satisfied. "What is the meaning of this?" said Candide; "and what demon is it that exercises his dominion all over the globe?"

He inquired who the stout gentleman was that was killed with so much ceremony. "He is an admiral," replied some of them.

"And why was this admiral killed?" "Because," said they, "he did not kill men enough himself. He attacked the French admiral, and was found guilty of not being near enough to him." "But then," said Candide, "was not the French admiral as far off from the English admiral, as he was from him?" "That is what cannot be doubted," replied they. "But in this country it is of very great service to kill an admiral now and then, in order to make the rest fight better."

Candide was so astonished and shocked at what he had seen and heard, that he would not set foot on shore, but agreed with the master of the Dutch vessel (though he was sure to be robbed by him, as he had been by his countryman at Surinam) to carry him directly to Venice.

The master was ready in two days. They coasted all along France. Passing within sight of Lisbon, Candide gave a very deep groan.

They passed the Straits, entered the Mediterranean, and at last arrived at Venice.

"The Lord be praised," said Candide, embracing Martin, "it is here that I shall see the fair Cunegonde again! I have as good an opinion of Cacambo, as of myself. Everything is right, everything goes well; everything is the best that it can possibly be."

CHAPTER XXIV

Concerning Paquetta and Girofflee

As soon as they arrived at Venice, he caused search for Cacambo in all the inns, in all the coffeehouses, and among all the girls of the town, but could not find him. He sent every day to all the ships and barks that arrived; but no news of Cacambo. "Well," said he to Martin, "I have had time enough to go from Surinam to Bordeaux, from Bordeaux to Paris, from Paris to Dieppe, from Dieppe to Portsmouth; after that I have coasted along Portugal and Spain, and traversed the Mediterranean, and have now been some months at Venice, and yet, for all that, the lovely Cunegonde is not come. Instead of her, I have only met with a cheating hussy, and a treacherous man of Périgord. Cunegonde is certainly dead, and I have nothing to do but to die also. Ah! it would have been far better for me to have stayed in that paradise, Dorado, than to have returned again to this cursed Europe. You are certainly right, my dear Martin, all is illusion and misery here."

He fell into a deep melancholy, and never frequented the opera, or the other diversions of the carnival; nay, he was proof against all the charms of the fair sex. Martin said to him, "You are very simple indeed, to fancy that a mongrel valet, with five or six millions in his pocket, would go to the end of the world in quest of your mistress, and bring her to Venice. If he meets with her, he'll keep her for himself; if he cannot find her, he'll get somebody else. Let me advise you to forget both your valet Cacambo, and your mistress Cunegonde." Martin was a most wretched comforter. The melancholy of Candide increased; and Martin never ceased preaching that there was but very little virtue, and as little happiness, to be found on earth, excepting, perhaps, at Eldorado, where it was almost impossible for anyone to go.

Whilst they were disputing on this important subject, and waiting for Cunegonde, Candide perceived a young guard in the Place St. Mark, with his arm around a young girl. He looked fresh, plump, and full of vigor; his eyes were sparkling, his air bold, his mien lofty, and his gait firm. This girl was tolerably handsome, and was singing a song; she ogled her companion with a great deal of passion, and now and then would give his fat cheeks a pinch.

"At least, you will grant me," said Candide to Martin, "that these two folks are happy. I have never found any but unhappy wretches till now, all over this habitable globe, excepting at Eldorado; but as for the girl and the guard, I will lay any wager that they are as happy as happy can be." "I will lay a wager that they are not," said Martin. "Let us invite them to dinner," said Candide, "then we shall see whether I am mistaken or not."

He immediately accosted them, made them a bow, and invited them to his inn to eat macaroni, partridges of Lombardy, and caviare, and to drink montepulciano, Cyprus and Samos wine. The girl blushed; the guard accepted the invitation, and the girl followed him, looking at Candide with surprise and confusion, whilst the tears trickled down her cheeks. Scarce had she entered into Candide's room, when she said to him, "What! does not Mr. Candide know his old friend Paquetta again?" At these words, Candide, who had not yet looked at her with any degree of attention, because Cunegonde engrossed all his thoughts, said to her, "Ah! my poor girl, is it you? you, who reduced Dr. Pangloss to the dreadful plight in which I saw him?"

"Ah, Sir! 'tis I myself," said Paquetta; "I find you know the whole story; and I have been informed of all the terrible disasters which have happened to the family of my Lady the Baroness, and the fair Cunegonde. My fate, I assure you, has not been less melancholy. I was very innocent when you knew me. A cavalier easily seduced me. The effects of it were terrible. I was obliged to leave the castle sometime after the Baron kicked and thrust you out of the door. If a celebrated quack had not taken pity on me, I should have perished. I was the quack's mistress for some time by way of recompense. His wife, who was as jealous as the devil, beat me every day, most unmercifully; she was a very fiend of hell. The doctor was one of the ugliest fellows I ever saw in my life, and I one of the most wretched creatures that ever existed, to be beat every day for the sake of a man whom I hated. You know how dangerous it is for a jealous woman to be married to a doctor. Being quite exasperated with his wife's behavior, he gave her one day so efficacious a remedy to cure her of a slight cold she had, that she died two hours after in the most horrid convulsions. My mistress's relations entered a criminal action against my master; he took to his heels and I was carried to jail. My innocence would never have saved me, if I had not been so handsome. The Judge acquitted me, on condition of his succeeding the doctor. I was soon afterwards supplanted by a rival, driven out of doors without any recompense, and obliged to continue this abominable occupation, which appears so pleasant to you men, while it is to us women the very abyss of misery. I am come to practice my profession at Venice. Ah, Sir, if you could imagine what it is to be obliged to caress indifferently, an old merchant, a counsellor, a gondolier; to be exposed to all sorts of insults and outrages; to be often reduced to borrow a petticoat, to have it rudely pulled up by a disagreeable rascal; to be robbed by one gallant of what one has got from another; to be fleeced by the officers of justice, and to have nothing in prospect but a frightful old age, a hospital, and a dunghill for a sepulchre, you would confess that I am one of the most unfortunate creatures in the world."

Paquetta opened her mind in this manner to the good Candide, in his closet, in the presence of Martin; who said to Candide, "You see I have won half the wager already."

Girofflee waited in the dining-room, and drank a glass or two while he was waiting for dinner. "But," said Candide, to Paquetta, "you had an air so gay, so content, when I first met you, you sung, and caressed the guard with so much warmth, that you seemed to be as happy then as you pretend to be miserable now." "Ah, Sir," replied Paquetta, "this is one of the miseries of the trade. Yesterday, I was robbed and beaten by an officer, and to-day I am obliged to appear in good humor to please a guard." Candide wanted no more, to be satisfied, and he owned that Martin was in the right. They sat down to table with Paquetta and the soldier; the repast was very entertaining, and towards the end, they began to speak to each other with some degree of confidence. "My man," said Candide to the guard, "you seem to enjoy a state that all the world might look on with envy. The flower of health blossoms on your countenance, and your physiognomy speaks nothing but happiness; you have a very pretty girl to divert you, and you seem to be well satisfied with your station as a guard."

"Faith, Sir," said Girofflee, "I wish that all the guards were at the bottom of the sea. I have been tempted an hundred times to set fire to the camp, and go and turn Turk. My parents forced me, at the age of fifteen, to put on this cursed uniform, to increase the fortune of an elder brother of mine, whom God confound. Jealousy, discord, and fury, reside there. It is true, indeed, I have brought me in a little money; one part of which the commander robbed me of, and the rest serves me to spend with the girls; but every evening, when I enter the camp, I am ready to dash out my brains against the walls; and all the rest are in the same case."

Martin turned towards Candide, with his usual coolness, "Well," said he to him, "have not I won the whole wager now?" Candide gave two thousand piastres to Paquetta, and one thousand to Girofflee. "I'll answer for it," said he, "this will make them happy." "I don't believe a word of it," said Martin; "you may perhaps make them a great deal more miserable by your piastres." "Be that as it may," said Candide; "but one thing comforts me, I see that one often finds those persons whom one never expected to find anymore; and as I have found my red sheep and Paquetta again, it may be I may find Cunegonde again too." "I wish," said Martin, "that she may one day make you happy; but it is what I very much question." "You are very incredulous," said Candide. "That is what I always was," said Martin.

"But only look on these gondoliers," said Candide; "are they not perpetually singing?" "You don't see them at home with their wives, and their monkeys of children," said Martin. "The Doge has his inquietudes, and the gondoliers have theirs. Indeed, generally speaking, the condition of a gondolier is preferable to that of a doge; but I believe that the difference is so small, that it is not worth the trouble of examining into."

"People speak," said Candide, "of Seignior Pococurante, who lives in that fine palace upon the Brenta, and who entertains strangers in the most polite manner. They pretend that this man never felt any uneasiness." "I should be glad to see so extraordinary a phenomenon," said Martin. On which Candide instantly sent to Seignior Pococurante, to get permission to pay him a visit the next day.

CHAPTER XXV

The Visit to Seignior Pococurante, the Noble Venetian

Candide and Martin went in a gondola on the Brenta, and arrived at the palace of the noble Pococurante. His gardens were very spacious and ornamented with fine statues of marble, and the palace itself was a piece of excellent architecture. The master of the house, a very rich man, of about threescore, received our two inquisitives very politely, but with very little heartiness; which, though it confused Candide, did not give the least uneasiness to Martin.

At first, two young girls, handsome, and very neatly dressed, served them with chocolate, which was frothed extremely well. Candide could not help dropping them a compliment on their beauty, their politeness, and their address. "The creatures are well enough," said the senator Pococurante: "I sometimes make them sleep with me; for I am quite disgusted with the ladies of the town; their coquetry, their jealousies, quarrels, humors, monkey-tricks, pride, follies, and the sonnets one is obliged to make, or hire others to make for them; but, after all, these two girls begin to grow tiresome to me."

After breakfast, Candide, taking a walk in a long gallery, was charmed with the beauty of the pictures. He asked by what master were the two first. "They are by Raphael," said the senator; "I bought them at a very high price, merely out of vanity, some years ago. They are said to be the finest paintings in Italy: but they do not please me at all; the colors are dead, the figures not finished, and do not appear with *relief* enough; the drapery is very bad. In short, let people say what they will, I do not find there a true imitation of nature. I do not like a piece, unless it makes me think I see nature itself; but there are no such pieces to be met with. I have, indeed, a great many pictures, but I do not value them at all."

While they were waiting for dinner, Pococurante entertained them with a concert; Candide was quite charmed with the music. "This *noise*," said Pococurante, "might divert one for half an hour, or so; but if it were to last any longer, it would grow tiresome to everybody, though no soul durst own it. Music is, nowadays, nothing else but the art of executing difficulties; and what has nothing but difficulty to recommend it, does not please in the long run.

"I might, perhaps, take more pleasure in the opera, if they had not found out the secret of making such a monster of it as shocks me. Let those go that will to see wretched tragedies set to music, where the scenes are composed for no other end than to lug in by the head and ears two or three ridiculous songs, in order to show off the throat of an actress to advantage. Let who will, or can, swoon away with pleasure, at hearing a eunuch trill out the part of Caesar and Cato, while strutting upon the stage with a ridiculous and affected air. For my part, I have long ago bid adieu to those paltry entertainments, which constitute the glory of Italy, and are purchased so extravagantly dear." Candide disputed the point a little, but with great discretion. Martin was entirely of the same sentiments with the senator. They sat down to table, and after an excellent dinner, went into the library. Candide, casting his eyes upon a Homer very handsomely bound, praised his High Mightiness for the goodness of his taste. "There," said he, "is a book that was the delight of the good Pangloss, the greatest philosopher in Germany." "It doesn't delight me," said Pococurante, with utter indifference; "I was made to believe formerly, that I took a pleasure in reading Homer. But his continued repetition of battles that resemble each other; his gods, who are always very busy without bringing anything to a decision; his Helen, who is the subject of the war, and has scarce anything to do in the whole piece; I say all these defects give me the greatest disgust. I have asked some learned men, if they perused him with as little pleasure as I did? Those who were candid confessed to me, that they could not bear to touch the book, but that they were obliged to give it a place in their libraries, as a monument of antiquity, as they do old rusty medals, which are of no use in commerce."

"Your Excellence does not entertain the same opinion of Virgil?" said Candide. "I confess," replied Pococurante, "that the second, the fourth, and the sixth book of his Aeneid are excellent; but as for his pious Aeneas, his brave Cloanthus, his friend Achates, the little Ascanius, the infirm King Latinus, the burgess Amata, and the insipid Lavinia, I do not think anything can be more frigid or more disagreeable. I prefer Tasso, and Ariosto's soporiferous tales far before him."

"Shall I presume to ask you, sir," said Candide, "whether you do not enjoy a great deal of pleasure in perusing Horace?" "He has some maxims," said Pococurante, "which may be of a little service to a man who knows the world, and being delivered in expressive numbers, are imprinted more easily on the memory. But I set little value on his voyage to Brundusium, his description of his bad dinner, and the Billingsgate squabble between one Pupillus, whose speech, he said was full of filthy stuff, and another whose words were as sharp as vinegar. I never could read without great disgust, his indelicate lines against old women and witches; and I cannot see any merit in his telling his friend Maecenas, that if he should be ranked by him amongst the lyric poets, he would strike the stars with his sublime brow. Some fools admire everything in an author of reputation; for my part, I read only for myself; I approve nothing but what suits my own taste." Candide, having been taught to judge of nothing for himself, was very much surprised at what he heard; but Martin looked upon the sentiment of Pococurante as very rational.

"Oh, there's Cicero," said Candide; "this great man, I fancy, you are never tired of reading." "I never read him at all," replied the Venetian. "What is it to me, whether he pleads for Rabirius or Cluentius? I have trials enough of my own. I might, indeed, have been a greater friend to his philosophical works, but when I found he doubted of everything, I concluded I knew as much as he did, and that I had no need of a tutor to learn ignorance."

"Well! here are four and twenty volumes of the Academy of Sciences," cried Martin; "it is possible there may be something valuable in them." "There might be," said Pococurante, "if a single one of the authors of this hodgepodge had been even the inventor of the art of making pins; but there is nothing in all those volumes but chimerical systems, and scarce a single article of real use."

"What a prodigious number of theatrical pieces you have got here," said Candide, "in Italian, Spanish, and French!" "Yes," said the Senator, "there are about three thousand, and not three dozen good ones among them all. As for that collection of sermons, which all together are not worth one page of Seneca, and all those huge volumes of divinity, you may be sure they are never opened either by me or anybody else."

Martin perceiving some of the shelves filled with English books; "I fancy," said he, "a republican, as you are, must certainly be pleased with compositions that are writ with so great a degree of freedom." "Yes," said Pococurante, "it is commendable to write what one thinks; it is the privilege of man. But all over our Italy they write nothing but what they don't think. Those who now inhabit the country of the Caesars and Antonines, dare not have a single idea, without taking out a license from a Jacobin. I should be very well satisfied with the freedom that breathes in the English writers, if passion and the spirit of party did not corrupt all that was valuable in it."

Candide discovering a Milton, asked him if he did not look upon that author as a great genius? "What!" said Pococurante, "that blockhead, that has made a long commentary in ten books of rough verse, on the first chapter of Genesis? that gross imitator of the Greeks, who has disfigured the creation, and who, when Moses has represented the Eternal producing the world by a word, makes the Messiah take a large pair of compasses from the armory of God, to mark out his work? How can I have any esteem for one who has spoiled the hell and devils of Tasso; who turns Lucifer sometimes into a toad, and sometimes into a pigmy; makes him deliver the same speech a hundred times over; represents him disputing on divinity; and who, by a serious imitation of Ariosto's comic invention of firearms, represents the devils letting off their cannon in heaven? Neither myself, nor anyone else in Italy, can be pleased at these outrages against common sense; but the marriage of Sin and Death, and the adders of which Sin was brought to bed, are enough to make every person of the least delicacy or taste vomit. This obscure, fantastical, and disgusting poem was despised at its first publication; and I only treat the author now in the same manner as he was treated in his own country by his contemporaries. By the by, I speak what I think; and I give myself no uneasiness whether other people think as I do, or not."

Candide was vexed at this discourse; for he respected Homer, and was fond of Milton. "Ah!" said he, whispering to Martin, "I am very much afraid that this strange man has a sovereign contempt for our German poets." "There would be no great harm in that," said Martin. "Oh, what an extraordinary man!" said Candide, muttering to himself. "What a great genius is this Pococurante! nothing can please him."

After having thus reviewed all the books, they went down into the garden. Candide expatiated upon its beauties. "I never knew anything laid out in such bad taste," said the master; "we have nothing but trifles here; but a day or two hence, I shall have one laid out upon a more noble plan."

When our two inquisitives had taken their leave of his Excellency, "Now, surely," said Candide to Martin, "you will confess that he is one of the happiest men upon earth, for he is above everything that he has." "Do not you see," said Martin, "that he is disgusted with everything that he has? Plato has said a long time ago, that the best stomachs are not those which cast up all sorts of victuals." "But," said Candide, "is not there pleasure in criticising everything? in perceiving defects where other people fancy they see beauties?" "That is to say," replied Martin, "that there is pleasure in having no pleasure." "Ah, well," said Candide, "no person will be so happy as myself, when I see Miss Cunegonde again." "It is always best to hope," said Martin.

In the meantime, days and weeks passed away, but no Cacambo was to be found. And Candide was so immersed in grief, that he did not recollect that Paquetta and Girofflee never so much as once came to return him thanks.

cradle; my father and mother were imprisoned; I was brought up in prison. I have sometimes permission to travel, accompanied by two persons as guards; I am also come to pass the carnival at Venice."

The third said, "I am Charles Edward, King of England; my father ceded his rights to the throne to me. I have sought to defend them; eight hundred of my adherents had their hearts torn out alive, and their heads struck off. I myself have been in prison; I am going to Rome, to pay a visit to my father, who has been dethroned, as well as myself and my grandfather, and am come to Venice to celebrate the carnival."

The fourth then said, "I was King of Poland; the fortune of war has deprived me of my hereditary dominions; my father experienced the same reverse; I resign myself to providence, like the Sultan Achmet, the Emperor Ivan, and Charles Edward, whom God long preserve; and I am come to pass the carnival at Venice."

The fifth said, "I was King of Poland; I lost my kingdom twice; but providence has given me another government, in which I have done more good than all the kings of the Sarmatians put together, have been able to do on the banks of the Vistula. I resign myself to providence, and am come to pass the carnival at Venice."

It was now the sixth monarch's turn to speak. "Gentlemen," said he, "I am not so great a prince as any of you; but for all that, I have been a King, as well as the best of you. I am Theodore; I was elected King of Corsica; I was once called *Your Majesty*, but at present am scarce allowed the title of *Sir*. I have caused money to be coined, but am not master at present of a farthing. I have had two secretaries of state, but now have scarce a single servant. I have been myself on a throne, and have for some time lain upon straw in a common jail in London. I am afraid I shall meet with the same treatment here, although I came hither, like your Majesties, to pass the carnival at Venice."

The five other Kings heard this speech with a noble compassion. Each of them gave King Theodore twenty sequins to buy him some clothes and shirts, and Candide made him a present of a diamond worth two thousand sequins. "Who," said the five kings, "can this person be, who is able to give, and really has given an hundred times as much as either of us?" "Sir, are you also a king?" "No, gentlemen," said Candide, "nor have I any desire to be one."

At the instant they rose from the table, there arrived at the same inn, four Serene Highnesses, who had also lost their dominions by the fortune of war, and were come to pass the carnival at Venice. But Candide took no notice of these newcomers, his thoughts being wholly taken up with going to Constantinople in search of his dear Cunegonde.

CHAPTER XXVII

Candide's Voyage to Constantinople

THE FAITHFUL CACAMBO HAD ALREADY PREVAILED ON THE TURKish captain who was going to carry Sultan Achmet back again to Constantinople, to receive Candide and Martin on board. They both of them embarked, after they had prostrated themselves before his miserable Highness. As Candide was on his way, he said to Martin, "There were six dethroned kings that we supped with; and what is still more, among these six kings, there was one that I gave alms to. Perhaps there may be a great many other princes more unfortunate still. For my own part, I have lost only one hundred sheep, and am flying to the arms of Cunegonde. My dear Martin, I must still say, Pangloss was in the right; all things are for the best." "I wish they were," said Martin. "But," said Candide, "the adventure we met with at Venice is something romantic. Such a thing was never before either seen or heard of, that six dethroned kings should sup together at a common inn." "This is not more extraordinary," replied Martin, "than most of the things that have happened to us. It is a common thing for kings to be dethroned; and with respect to the honor that we had of supping with them, it is a trifle that does not merit our attention."

Scarce had Candide got on board, when he fell on the neck of his old servant and friend Cacambo. "Well," said he, "what news of Cunegonde? is she still a miracle of beauty? does she love me still? how does she do? No doubt but you have bought a palace for her at Constantinople?"

"My dear master," replied Cacambo, "Cunegonde washes dishes on the banks of the Propontis, for a prince who has very few to wash; she is a slave in the house of an ancient sovereign named *Ragotsky*, to whom the Grand Turk allows three crowns a day to support him in his asylum; but, what is worse than all, she has lost her beauty, and is become shockingly ugly." "Well, handsome or ugly," replied Candide, "I am a man of honor, and it is my duty to love her still. But how came she to be reduced to so abject a condition, with the five or six millions that you carried her?" "Well," said Cacambo, "was I not to give two millions to Signor Don Fernandes d'Obaraa, y Figuero, y Mascarenes, y Lampourdos, y Souza, the governor of Buenos Aires, for permission to take Miss Cunegonde back again? and did not a pirate rob us of all the rest? Did not this pirate carry us to Cape Matapan, to Milo, to Nicaria, to Samos, to Dardanelles, to Marmora, to Scutari? Cunegonde and the old woman are servants to the prince I told you of, and I am a slave of the dethroned sultan." "What a chain of shocking calamities!" said Candide. "But, after all, I have some diamonds, I shall easily purchase Cunegonde's liberty. It is a pity that she is grown so ugly."

Then, turning himself to Martin, "Who do you think," says he, "is most to be pitied: the Sultan Achmet, the Emperor Ivan, King Charles Edward, or myself?" "I cannot tell," said Martin, "I must look into your hearts to be able to tell." "Ah!" said Candide, "if Pangloss were here, he would know and tell us." "I know not," replied Martin, "in what sort of scales your Pangloss would weigh the misfortunes of mankind, and how he would appraise their sorrows. All that I can venture to say is, that there are millions of men upon earth a hundred times more to be pitied than King Charles Edward, the Emperor Ivan, or Sultan Achmet."

"That may be so," said Candide.

In a few days they reached the Black Sea. Candide began with ransoming Cacambo at an extravagant price; and, without loss of time, he got into a galley with his companions, to go to the banks of the Propontis, in search of Cunegonde, however ugly she might have become.

Among the crew, there were two slaves that rowed very badly, to whose bare shoulders the Levant trader would now and then apply severe strokes with a bull's pizzle. Candide, by a natural sympathy, looked at them more attentively than at the rest of the galley-slaves, and went up to them with a heart full of pity. The features of two of their faces, though very much disfigured, seemed to bear some resemblance to those of Pangloss, and the unfortunate Baron, the brother of Miss Cunegonde. This fancy made him feel very sad. He looked at them again more attentively. "Really," said he to Cacambo, "if I had not seen the good Pangloss hanged, and had not had the misfortune to kill the Baron myself, I should think it was they who are rowing in this galley."

At the names of the Baron and Pangloss, the two galley-slaves gave a loud shriek, became as if petrified in their seats, and let their oars drop. The master of the Levanter ran up to them, and redoubled the lashes of the bull's pizzle upon them. "Hold! hold! Signior," cried Candide, "I will give you what money you please." "What! it is Candide!" said one of the galley-slaves; "Oh! it is Candide!" said the other. "Do I dream?" said Candide; "am I awake? am I in this galley? is that Master Baron whom I killed? is that Master Pangloss whom I saw hanged?"

"It is ourselves! It is our very selves!" they exclaimed. "What! is that the great philosopher?" said Martin. "Harkee, Master Levant Captain," said Candide, "what will you take for the ransom of Monsieur Thunder-ten-tronckh, one of the first Barons of the empire, together with Master Pangloss, the most profound metaphysician of Germany?" "You Christian dog," said the Levant captain, "since these two dogs of Christian slaves are a baron and a metaphysician, which, without doubt, are high dignitaries in their own country, you shall give me fifty thousand sequins." "You shall have the money, sir; carry me back again, like lightning, to Constantinople, and you shall be paid directly. But stop, carry me to Miss Cunegonde first." The Levant captain, on the first offer of

Candide, had turned the head of the vessel towards the city, and made the other slaves row faster than a bird cleaves the air.

Candide embraced the Baron and Pangloss a hundred times. "How happened it that I did not kill you, my dear Baron? and, my dear Pangloss, how came you to life again, after being hanged? and how came both of you to be galley-slaves in Turkey?" "Is it true that my dear sister is in this country?" said the Baron. "Yes," replied Cacambo. "Then I see my dear Candide once more," said Pangloss.

Candide presented Martin and Cacambo to them; the whole party mutually embraced, and all spoke at the same time. The galley flew like lightning, and they were already in the port. A Jew was sent for, to whom Candide sold a diamond for fifty thousand sequins, which was worth a hundred thousand, the Israelite swearing by Abraham that he could not give any more. He immediately paid the ransom of the Baron and Pangloss. The latter threw himself at the feet of his deliverer, and bathed them with his tears; as for the other, he thanked him with a nod, and promised to repay him the money the first opportunity. "But is it possible that my sister is in Turkey?" said he. "Nothing is more possible," replied Cacambo; "for she scours dishes in the house of a prince of Transylvania!" Two more Jews were instantly sent for, to whom Candide sold some more diamonds; and he and his party all set out again, in another galley, to go and deliver Cunegonde.

CHAPTER XXVIII

What Happened to Candide, Cunegonde, Pangloss, Martin, Etc.

"I ASK YOUR PARDON ONCE MORE," SAID CANDIDE TO THE BARON. "I ask pardon for having thrust my sword through your body." "Don't let us say any more about it," said the Baron; "I was a little too hasty, I must confess. But since you desire to know by what fatality I came to be a galley-slave, I will inform you. After I was cured of my wound, by a brother who was apothecary, I was attacked and carried off by a party of Spaniards, who confined me in prison at Buenos Aires, at the very time my sister was setting out from thence. I demanded leave to return to Europe. I was nominated to go as almoner to Constantinople, with the French ambassador. I had not been eight days engaged in this employment, when one day I met with a young, well-made Icoglan. It was then very hot; the young man went to bathe himself, and I took the opportunity to bathe myself too. I did not know that it was a capital crime for a Christian to be found naked with a young Mussulman. A cadi ordered me to receive a hundred strokes of the bastinado on the soles of my feet, and condemned me to the galleys. I do not think there ever was a greater act of injustice. But I should be glad to know how it comes about, that my sister is dish-washer in the kitchen of a Transylvania prince, who is a refugee among the Turks."

"But you, my dear Pangloss," said Candide, how came I ever to set eyes on you again!" "It is true, indeed," said Pangloss, "that you saw me hanged; I ought naturally to have been burnt; but you may remember, that it rained prodigiously when they were going to roast me; the storm was so violent that they despaired of lighting the fire. I was therefore hanged because they could do no better. A surgeon bought my body, carried it home with him, and began to dissect me. He first made a crucial incision. No one could have been more slovenly hanged than I was. The executioner of the inquisition burnt people marvellously well, but he was not used to the art of hanging them. The cord being wet did not slip properly, and the noose was badly tied: in short, I still drew my breath. The crucial incision made me give such a dreadful shriek, that my surgeon fell down backwards, and fancying he was dissecting the devil, he ran away, ready to die with the fright, and fell down a second time on the stair-case, as he was making off. His wife ran out of an adjacent closet, on hearing the noise, saw me extended on the table with my crucial incision, and being more frightened than her husband, fled also, and tumbled over him. When they were come to themselves a little, I heard the surgeon's wife say to him, My dear, how came you to be so foolish as to venture to dissect a heretic? Don't you know that the devil always takes possession of the bodies of such people? I will go immediately and fetch a priest to exorcise him. I shuddered at this proposal, and mustered up what little strength I had left to cry out, Oh! have pity upon me! At length the Portuguese barber took courage, sewed up my skin, and his wife nursed me so well, that I was upon my feet again in about fifteen days. The barber got me a place, to be footman to a knight of Malta, who was going to Venice; but my master not being able to pay me my wages, I engaged in the service of a Venetian merchant, and went along with him to Constantinople."

"One day I took a fancy to go into a mosque. There was nobody there but an old iman, and a very handsome young devotee saying her prayers. Her breast was uncovered; she had in her bosom a beautiful nosegay of tulips, anemonies, ranunculuses, hyacinths, and auriculas; she let her nosegay fall; I took it up, and presented it to her with the most profound reverence. However, I was so long in handing it to her, that the iman fell into a passion, and seeing

I was a Christian, called out for help. They carried me before the cadi, who ordered me a hundred bastinadoes, and to be sent to the galleys. I was chained to the same galley and the same bench with the Baron. There were on board this galley, four young men from Marseilles, five Neapolitan priests, and two monks of Corfu, who told us that the like adventures happened every day. The Baron pretended that he had suffered more injustice than I; and I insisted that it was far more innocent to put a nosegay into a young woman's bosom, than to be found stark naked with an Icoglan. We were perpetually disputing, and we received twenty lashes every day with a bull's pizzle, when the concatenation of events in this universe brought you to our galley, and you ransomed us."

"Well, my dear Pangloss," said Candide, "when you were hanged, dissected, severely beaten, and tugging at the oar in the galley, did you always think, that things in this world were all for the best?" "I am still as I always have been, of my first opinion," answered Pangloss; "for as I am a philosopher, it would be inconsistent with my character to contradict myself; especially as Leibnitz could not be in the wrong; and his pre-established harmony is certainly the finest system in the world, as well as his gross and subtle matter."

CHAPTER XXIX

How Candide Found Cunegonde and the Old Woman Again

WHILE CANDIDE, THE BARON, PANGLOSS, MARTIN, AND CACAMBO, were relating their adventures to each other, and disputing about the contingent and non-contingent events of this world, and while they were arguing upon effects and causes, on moral and physical evil, on liberty and necessity, and on the consolations a person may experience in the galleys in Turkey, they arrive on the banks of the Propontis, at the house of the Prince of Transylvania. The first objects which presented themselves were Cunegonde and the old woman, hanging out some table-linen on the line to dry.

The Baron grew pale at this sight. Even Candide, the affectionate lover, on seeing his fair Cunegonde awfully tanned, with her eyelids reversed, her neck withered, her cheeks wrinkled, her arms red and rough, was seized with horror, jumped near three yards backwards, but afterwards advanced to her, but with more politeness than passion. She embraced Candide and her brother, who, each of them, embraced the old woman, and Candide ransomed them both.

There was a little farm in the neighborhood, which the old woman advised Candide to hire, till they could meet with better accommodations for their whole company. As Cunegonde did not know that she had grown ugly, nobody having told her of it, she put Candide in mind of his promise to marry her, in so peremptory a manner, that he durst not refuse her. But when this thing was intimated to the Baron: "I will never suffer," said he, "such meanness on her part, nor such insolence on yours. With this infamy I will never be reproached. The children of my sister shall never be enrolled in the chapters of Germany. No; my sister shall never marry any but a Baron of the empire. Cunegonde threw herself at her brother's feet, and bathed them with her tears, but he remained inflexible. "You ungrateful puppy, you," said Candide to him, "I have delivered you from the galleys; I have paid your ransom; I have also paid that of your sister, who was a scullion here, and is very homely; I have the goodness, however, to make her my wife, and you are fool enough to oppose it; I have a good mind to kill you again, you make me so angry." "You may indeed kill me again," said the Baron; "but you shall never marry my sister, while I have breath."

CHAPTER XXX

Conclusion

Candide had no great desire, at the bottom of his heart, to marry Cunegonde. But the extreme impertinence of the Baron determined him to conclude the match, and Cunegonde pressed it so earnestly, that he could not retract. He advised with Pangloss, Martin, and the trusty Cacambo. Pangloss drew up an excellent memoir, in which he proved, that the Baron had no right over his sister, and that she might, according to all the laws of the empire, espouse Candide with her left hand. Martin was for throwing the Baron into the sea: Cacambo was of opinion that it would be best to send him back again to the Levant captain, and make him work at the galleys. This advice was thought good; the old woman approved it, and nothing was said to his sister about it. The scheme was put in execution for a little money, and so they had the pleasure of punishing the pride of a German Baron.

It is natural to imagine that Candide, after so many disasters, married to his sweetheart, living with the philosopher Pangloss, the philosopher Martin, the discreet Cacambo, and the old woman, and especially as he had brought so many diamonds from the country of the ancient Incas, must live the most agreeable life of any man in the whole world. But he had been so cheated by the Jews, that he had nothing left but the small farm; and his wife, growing still more ugly, turned peevish and insupportable. The old woman was very infirm, and worse humored than Cunegonde herself. Cacambo, who worked in the garden, and went to Constantinople to sell its productions, was worn out with labor, and cursed his fate. Pangloss was ready to despair, because he did not shine at the head of some university in Germany. As for Martin, as he was firmly persuaded that all was equally bad throughout, he bore things with patience. Candide, Martin, and Pangloss, disputed sometimes about metaphysics and ethics. They often saw passing under the windows of the farmhouse boats full of effendis, bashaws, and cadis, who were going into banishment to Lemnos, Mitylene, and Erzerum. They observed that other cadis, other bashaws, and other effendis, succeeded in the posts of those who were exiled, only to be banished themselves in turn. They saw heads nicely impaled, to be presented to the Sublime Porte. These spectacles increased the number of their disputations; and when they were not disputing, their *ennui* was so tiresome that the old woman would often say to them, "I want to know which is the worst;—to be ravished an hundred times by negro pirates, to run the gauntlet among the Bulgarians, to be whipped and hanged, to be dissected, to row in the galleys; in a word, to have suffered all the miseries we have undergone, or to stay here, without doing anything?" "That is a great question," said Candide.

This discourse gave rise to new reflections, and Martin concluded upon the whole, that mankind were born to live either in the distractions of inquietude, or in the lethargy of disgust. Candide did not agree with that opinion, but remained in a state of suspense. Pangloss confessed, that he had always suffered dreadfully; but having once maintained that all things went wonderfully well, he still kept firm to his hypothesis, though it was quite opposed to his real feelings.

What contributed to confirm Martin in his shocking principles, to make Candide stagger more than ever, and to embarrass Pangloss, was, that one day they saw Paquetta and Girofflee, who were in the greatest distress, at their farm. They had quickly squandered away their three thousand piastres, had parted, were reconciled, quarrelled again, had been confined in prison, had made their escape, and Girofflee had at length turned Turk. Paquetta continued her trade wherever she went, but made nothing by it. "I could easily foresee," said Martin to Candide, "that your presents would soon be squandered away, and would render them more miserable. You and Cacambo have spent millions of piastres, and are not a bit happier than Girofflee and Paquetta." "Ha! ha!" said Pangloss to Paquetta, "has Providence then brought you amongst us again, my poor child? Know, then, that you have cost me the tip of my nose, one eye, and one of my ears, as you see. What a world this is!" This new adventure set them a philosophizing more than ever.

There lived in the neighborhood a very famous dervish, who passed for the greatest philosopher in Turkey. They went to consult him. Pangloss was chosen speaker, and said to him, "Master, we are come to desire you would tell us, why so strange an animal as man was created."

"What's that to you?" said the dervish; "is it any business of thine?" "But, my reverend father," said Candide, "there is a horrible amount of evil in the world." "What signifies," said the dervish, "whether there be good or evil? When his Sublime Highness send a vessel to Egypt, does it trouble him, whether the mice on board are at their ease or not?" "What would you have one do then?" said Pangloss. "Hold your tongue," said the dervish. "I promised myself the pleasure," said Pangloss, "of reasoning with you upon effects and causes, the best of possible worlds, the origin of evil, the nature of the soul, and the pre-established harmony."—The dervish, at these words, shut the door in their faces.

During this conference, news was brought that two viziers and a mufti were strangled at Constantinople, and a great many of their friends impaled. This catastrophe made a great noise for several hours. Pangloss, Candide, and Martin, on their way back to the little farm, met a good-looking old man, taking the air at his door, under an arbor of orange trees. Pangloss, who had as much curiosity as philosophy, asked him the name of the mufti who was lately strangled. "I know nothing at all about it," said the good man; "and what's more, I never knew the name of a single mufti, or a single vizier, in my life. I am an entire stranger to the story you mention; and presume that, generally speaking, they who trouble their heads with state affairs, sometimes die shocking deaths, not without deserving it. But I never trouble my head about what is doing at Constantinople; I content myself with sending my fruits thither, the produce of my garden, which I cultivate with my own hands!" Having said these words, he introduced the strangers into his house. His two daughters and two sons served them with several kinds of sherbet, which they made themselves, besides caymac, enriched with the peels of candied citrons, oranges, lemons, ananas, pistachio nuts, and Mocoa coffee, unadulterated with the bad coffee of Batavia and the isles. After which, the two daughters of this good Mussulman perfumed the beards of Candide, Pangloss, and Martin.

"You must certainly," said Candide to the Turk, "have a very large and very opulent estate!" "I have only twenty acres," said the Turk; "which I, with my children, cultivate. Labor keeps us free from three of the greatest evils: tiresomeness, vice, and want."

As Candide returned to his farm, he made deep reflections on the discourse of the Turk. Said he to Pangloss and Martin, "The condition of this good old man seems to me preferable to that of the six kings with whom we had the honor to sup." "The grandeurs of royalty," said Pangloss, "are very precarious, in the opinion of all philosophers. For, in short, Eglon, king of the Moabites, was assassinated by Ehud; Absalom was hung by the hair of his head, and pierced through with three darts; King Nadab, the son of Jeroboam, was killed by Baasha; King Elah by Zimri; Ahaziah by Jehu; Athaliah by Jehoiadah; the kings Joachim, Jechonias, and Zedekias, were carried into captivity. You know the fates of Croesus, Astyages, Darius, Dionysius of Syracuse, Pyrrhus, Perseus, Hannibal, Jugurtha, Ariovistus, Caesar, Pompey, Nero, Otho, Vitellius, Domitian, Richard II, Edward II, Henry VI, Richard III, Mary Stuart, Charles I of England, the three Henrys of France, and the Emperor Henry IV. You know——" "I know very well," said Candide, "that we ought to look after our garden." "You are in the right," said Pangloss, "for when man was placed in the garden of Eden, he was placed there, *ut operatur eum,* to cultivate it; which proves that mankind are not created to be idle." "Let us work," said Martin, "without disputing; it is the only way to render life supportable."

All their little society entered into this laudable design, according to their different abilities. Their little piece of ground produced a plentiful crop. Cunegonde was indeed very homely, but she became an excellent pastry cook. Paquetta worked at embroidery, and the old woman took care of the linen. There was no idle person in the company, not excepting even Girofflee; he made a very good carpenter, and became a very honest man.

As to Pangloss, he evidently had a lurking consciousness that his theory required unceasing exertions, and all his ingenuity, to sustain it. Yet he stuck to it to the last; his thinking and talking faculties could hardly be diverted from it for a moment. He seized every occasion to say to Candide, "All the events in this best of possible worlds are admirably connected. If a single link in the great chain were omitted, the harmony of the entire universe would be destroyed. If you had not been expelled from that beautiful castle, with those cruel kicks, for your love to Miss Cunegonde; if you had not been imprisoned by the inquisition; if you had not travelled over a great portion of America on foot; if you had not plunged your sword through the Baron; if you had not lost all the sheep you brought from that fine country, Eldorado, together with the riches with which they were laden, you would not be here to-day, eating preserved citrons, and pistachio nuts."

"That's very well said, and may all be true," said Candide; "but let's cultivate our garden."

L'INGÉNU:
OR, THE
SINCERE HURON

CHAPTER I

The Huron Arrives in France

One day, Saint Dunstan, an Irishman by nation, left Ireland and took his route toward the coast of France, and set his saintship down in the bay of St. Malo.

Here St. Dunstan laid the foundation of a small priory, and gave it the name of the Priory Mountain, which it still keeps, as everybody knows.

In the year 1689, the fifteenth day of July, in the evening, the abbot Kerkabon, Prior of the Mountain, happened to take the air along the shore with Miss Kerkabon, his sister. The Prior, who was becoming aged, was a very good clergyman, beloved by his neighbors.

Miss Kerkabon, who had never been married, notwithstanding her hearty wishes so to be, had preserved a freshness of complexion in her forty-fifth year. Her character was that of a good and sensible woman. She was fond of pleasure, and was a devotee.

As they were walking, the Prior, looking on the sea, said to his sister:

"It was here, alas! that our poor brother embarked with our dear sister-in-law, Madam Kerkabon, his wife, on board the frigate 'Swallow,' in 1669, to serve the king in Canada. Had he not been killed, probably he would have written to us."

"Do you believe," says Miss Kerkabon, "that our sister-in-law has been eaten by the Cherokees, as we have been told?"

"Certain it is, had she not been killed, she would have come back. I shall weep for her all my lifetime. She was a charming woman; and our brother, who had a great deal of wit, would no doubt have made a fortune."

Thus were they going on with mutual tenderness, when they beheld a small vessel enter the bay of Rence with the tide. It was from England, and came to sell provisions. The crew leaped on shore without looking at the Prior or Miss, his sister, who were shocked at the little attention shown them.

That was not the behavior of a well-made youth, who, darting himself over the heads of his companions, stood on a sudden before Miss Kerkabon. Being unaccustomed to bowing, he made her a sign with his head. His figure and his dress attracted the notice of brother and sister. His head was uncovered, and his legs bare. Instead of shoes, he wore a kind of sandals. From his head his long hair flowed in tresses. A small close doublet displayed the beauty of his shape. He had a sweet and martial air. In one hand he held a small bottle of Barbados water, and in the other a bag, in which he had a goblet, and some sea biscuit. He spoke French very intelligibly. He offered some of his Barbados to Miss Kerkabon and her brother. He drank with them, he made them drink a second time, and all this with an air of such native simplicity, that quite charmed brother and sister. They offered him their service, and asked him who he was, and whither going? The young man answered: That he knew not where he should go; that he had some curiosity; that he had a desire to see the coast of France; that he had seen it, and should return.

The Prior, judging by his accent that he was not an Englishman, took the liberty of asking of what country he was.

"I am a Huron," answered the youth.

Miss Kerkabon, amazed and enchanted to see a Huron who had behaved so politely to her, begged the young man's company to supper. He complied immediately, and all three went together to the Priory of Our Lady of the Mountain. This short and round Miss devoured him with her little eyes, and said from time to time to her brother:

"This tall lad has a complexion of lilies and roses. What a fine skin he has for a Huron!"

"Very true, sister," says the Prior.

She put a hundred questions, one after another, and the traveller answered always pertinently.

The report was soon spread that there was a Huron at the Priory. All the genteel company of the country came to supper. The abbot of St. Yves came with Miss, his sister, a fine, handsome, well-educated girl. The bailiff, the tax-gatherer, and their wives, came all together. The foreigner was seated between Miss Kerkabon and Miss St. Yves. The company eyed him with admiration. They all questioned him together. This did not confound the Huron. He seemed to have taken Lord Bolingbroke's motto, *Nil admirari*. But at last tired out with so much noise, he told them in a sweet, but serious tone:

"Gentlemen, in my country one talks after another. How can I answer you, if you will not allow me to hear you?"

Reasoning always brings people to a momentary reflection. They were all silent.

Mr. Bailiff, who always made a property of a foreigner wherever he found him, and who was the first man for asking questions in the province, opening a mouth of large size, began:

"Sir, what is your name?"

"I have always been called the *Ingénu*," answered the Huron; "and the English have confirmed that name, because I always speak as I think, and act as I like."

"But, being born a Huron, how could you come to England?"

"I have been carried thither. I was made prisoner by the English after some resistance, and the English, who love brave people, because they are as brave and honest as we, proposed to me, either to return to my family, or go with them to England. I accepted the latter, having naturally a relish for travelling."

"But, sir," says the bailiff, with his usual gravity, "how could you think of abandoning father and mother?"

"Because I never knew either father or mother," says the foreigner.

This moved the company; they all repeated:

"Neither father nor mother!"

"We will be in their stead," says the mistress of the house, to her brother, the Prior: "How interesting this Huron gentleman is!"

The *Ingénu* thanked her with a noble and proud cordiality, and gave her to understand, that he wanted the assistance of nobody.

"I perceive, Mr. Huron," said the huge bailiff, "that you talk better French than can be expected from an Indian."

"A Frenchman," answered he, "whom they had made prisoner when I was a boy, and with whom I contracted a great friendship, taught it me. I rapidly learn what I like to learn. When I came to Plymouth, I met with one of your French refugees, whom you, I know not why, call Huguenots. He improved my knowledge of your language; and as soon as I could express myself intelligibly, I came to see your country, because I like the French well enough, if they do not put too many questions."

Notwithstanding this candid remark, the Abbé of St. Yves asked him, which of the three languages pleased him best, the Huron, English, or French?

"The Huron, to be sure," answered the *Ingénu.*

"Is it possible?" cried Miss Kerkabon. "I always thought the French was the first of all languages, after that of Low Brittany."

Then all were eager to know how, in Huron, they asked for snuff? He replied:

"Taya."

"What signifies to eat?"

"Essenten."

Miss Kerkabon was impatient to know how they called, to make love?

He informed her, *Trovander*; and insisted on it, not without reason, that these words were well worth their synonyms in French and English. *Trovander*, especially, seemed very pretty to all the company. The Prior, who had in his library a Huron grammar, which had been given him, rose from the table to consult it. He returned quite panting with tenderness and joy. He acknowledged the foreigner for a true Huron. The company speculated a little on the multiplicity of languages; and all agreed that had it not been for the unfortunate affair of the Tower of Babel, all the world would have spoken French.

The inquisitive bailiff, who till then had some suspicions of the foreigner, conceived the deepest respect for him. He spoke to him with more civility than before, and the Huron took no notice of it.

Miss St. Yves was very curious to know how people made love among the Hurons.

"In performing great actions to please such as resemble you."

All the company admired and applauded. Miss St. Yves blushed, and was extremely well pleased. Miss Kerkabon blushed likewise, but was not so well pleased. She was a little piqued that this gallantry was not addressed to her; but she was so good-natured, that her affection for the Huron was not diminished at all. She asked him, with great complacency, how many mistresses he had at home.

"Only one," answered the foreigner; "Miss Abacaba, the good friend of my dear nurse. The reed is not straighter, nor is ermine whiter,—no lamb meeker, no eagle fiercer, nor a stag swifter, than was my Abacaba. One day she pursued a hare not above fifty leagues from my habitation: a base Algonquin, who dwells an hundred leagues further, took her hare from her. I was told of it; I ran thither, and with one stroke of my club leveled him with the ground. I brought him to the feet of my mistress, bound hand and foot. Abacaba's parents were for burning him, but I always had a disrelish for such scenes. I set him at liberty. I made him my friend. Abacaba was so pleased with my conduct, that she preferred me to all her lovers. And she would have continued to love me, had she not been devoured by a bear! I slew the bear, and wore his skin a long while; but that has not comforted me."

Miss St. Yves felt a secret pleasure at hearing that Abacaba had been his only mistress, and that she was no more; yet she understood not the cause of her own pleasure. All eyes were riveted on the Huron, and he was much applauded for delivering an Algonquin from the cruelty of his countrymen.

The merciless bailiff had now grown so furious, that he even asked the Huron what religion he was of; whether he had chosen the English, the French, or that of the Huguenots?

"I am of my own religion," said he, "just as you are of yours."

"Lord!" cried Miss Kerkabon, "I see already that those wretched English have not once thought of baptizing him!"

"Good heavens," said Miss Yves, "how is it possible?"

The Huron assured her, that no true American had ever changed his opinion, and that there was not in their language a word to express inconstancy.

These last words extremely pleased Miss St. Yves.

"Oh! we'll baptize him, we'll baptize him," said Miss Kerkabon to the Prior. "You shall have that honor, my dear brother, and I will be his godmother. The Abbot St. Yves shall present him to the font. It will make a fine appearance: it will be talked of all over Brittany, and do us the greatest honor."

The company were all of the same mind with the mistress of the house; they all cried:

"We'll baptize him."

The Huron interrupted them by saying, that in England everyone was allowed to live as he pleased. He rather showed some aversion to the proposal which was made, and could not help telling them, that the laws of the Hurons were to the full as good as those of Low Brittany. He finished with saying, that he should return the next day. The bottles grew empty, and the company went to bed.

After the Huron had been conducted to his room, they saw that he spread the blankets on the floor, and laid himself down upon them in the finest attitude in the world.

CHAPTER II

The Huron, Called the Ingénu, *Acknowledged by His Relations*

THE *INGÉNU*, ACCORDING TO CUSTOM, AWOKE WITH THE SUN, AT the crowing of the cock, which is called in England and Huronia, "the trumpet of the day." He did not imitate what is styled good company, who languish in the bed of indolence till the sun has performed half its daily journey, unable to sleep, but not disposed to rise, and lose so many precious hours in that doubtful state between life and death, and who nevertheless complain that life is too short.

He had already traversed two or three leagues, and killed fifteen brace of game with his rifle, when, upon his return, he found the Prior of the Lady of the Mountain, with his discreet sister, walking in their little garden. He presented them with the spoils of his morning labor, and taking from his bosom a kind of little talisman, which he constantly wore about his neck, he entreated them to accept of it as an acknowledgment for the kind reception they had given him.

"It is," said he, "the most valuable thing I am possessed of. I have been assured that I shall always be happy whilst I carry this little toy about me; and I give it you that you may be always happy."

The Prior and Miss smiled with pity at the frankness of the *Ingénu*. This present consisted of two little portraits, poorly executed, and tied together with a greasy string.

Miss Kerkabon asked him, if there were any painters in Huronia?

"No," replied the *Ingénu,* "I had this curiosity from my nurse. Her husband had obtained it by conquest, in stripping some of the French of Canada, who had made war upon us. This is all I know of the matter."

The Prior looked attentively upon these pictures, whilst he changed color; his hands trembled, and he seemed much affected.

"By our Lady of the Mountain," he cried out, "I believe these to be the faces of my brother, the captain, and his lady."

Miss, after having consulted them with the like emotion, thought the same. They were both struck with astonishment and joy blended with grief. They both melted, they both wept, their hearts throbbed, and during their disorder, the pictures were interchanged between them at least twenty times in a second. They seemed to devour the Huron's pictures with their eyes. They asked one after another, and even both at once, at what time, in what place, and how these miniatures fell into the hands of the nurse? They reckoned and computed the time from the captain's departure: they recollected having received notice that he had penetrated as far as the country of the Hurons; and from that time they had never heard anything more of him.

The Huron had told them, that he had never known either father or mother. The Prior, who was a man of sense, observed that he had a little beard, and he knew very well that the Hurons never had any. His chin was somewhat hairy; he was therefore the son of an European. My brother and sister-in-law were never seen after the expedition against the Hurons, in 1669. My nephew must then have been nursing at the breast. The Huron nurse has preserved his life, and been a mother to him. At length, after an hundred questions and answers, the Prior and his sister concluded that the Huron was their own nephew. They embraced him, whilst tears streamed from their eyes: and the Huron laughed to think that an Indian should be nephew to a prior of Lower Brittany.

All the company went downstairs. Mr. de St. Yves, who was a great physiognomist, compared the two pictures with the Huron's countenance. They observed, very skillfully, that he had the mother's eyes, the forehead and nose of the late Captain Kerkabon, and the cheeks common to both.

Miss St. Yves, who had never seen either father or mother, was strenuously of opinion, that the young man had a perfect resemblance of them. They all admired Providence, and wondered at the strange events of this world. In a word, they were so persuaded, so convinced of the birth of the Huron, that he himself consented to be the Prior's nephew, saying, that he would as soon have him for his uncle as another.

The Prior went to return thanks in the church of Our Lady of the Mountain; whilst the Huron, with an air of indifference, amused himself with drinking in the house.

The English who had brought him over, and who were ready to set sail, came to tell him that it was time to depart.

"Probably," said he to them, "you have not met with any of your uncles and aunts. I shall stay here. Go you back to Plymouth. I give you all my clothes, as I have no longer occasion for anything in this world, since I am the nephew of a prior."

The English set sail, without being at all concerned whether the Huron had any relations or not in Lower Brittany.

After the uncle, the aunt, and the company had rejoiced; after the bailiff had once more overwhelmed the Huron with questions; after they had exhausted all their astonishment, joy, and tenderness, the Prior of the Mountain and the Abbé of St. Yves concluded that the Huron should be baptized with all possible expedition. But the case was very different with a tall robust Indian of twenty-two, and an infant who is regenerated without his knowing anything of the matter. It was necessary to instruct him, and this appeared difficult; for the Abbé of St. Yves supposed that a man who was not born in France, could not be endowed with common sense.

The Prior, indeed, observed to the company, that though, in fact, the ingenious gentleman, his nephew, was not so fortunate as to be born in Lower Brittany, he was not, upon that account, any way deficient in sense; which might be concluded from all his answers; and that, doubtless, nature had greatly favored him, as well on his father's as on his mother's side.

He then was asked if he had ever read any books? He said, he had read Rabelais translated into English, and some passages in Shakespeare, which he knew by heart; that these books belonged to the captain, on board of whose ship he came from America to Plymouth; and that he was very well pleased with them. The bailiff failed not to put many questions to him concerning these books.

"I acknowledge," said the Huron, "I thought, in reading them, I understood some things, but not the whole."

The Abbé of St. Yves reflected upon this discourse, that it was in this manner he had always read, and that most men read no other way.

"You have," said he, to the Huron, "doubtless read the Bible?"

"Never, Mr. Abbé: it was not among the captain's books. I never heard it mentioned."

"This is the way with those cursed English," said Miss Kerkabon; "they think more of a play of Shakespeare's, a plum pudding, or a bottle of rum, than they do of the Pentateuch. For this reason they have never converted any Indians in America. They are certainly cursed by God; and we shall conquer Jamaica and Virginia from them in a very short time."

Be this as it may, the most skillful tailor in all St. Malo was sent for to dress the Huron from head to foot. The company separated, and the bailiff went elsewhere to display his inquisitiveness. Miss St. Yves, in parting, returned several times to observe the young stranger, and made him lower curtsies than ever she did anyone in her life.

The bailiff, before he took his leave, presented to Miss St. Yves a stupid dolt of a son, just come from college; but she scarce looked at him, so much was she taken up with the politeness of the Huron.

CHAPTER III

The Huron Converted

THE PRIOR FINDING THAT HE WAS SOMEWHAT ADVANCED IN YEARS, and that God had sent him a nephew for his consolation, took it into his head that he would resign his benefice in his favor, if he succeeded in baptizing him and of making him enter into orders.

The Huron had an excellent memory. A good constitution, inherited from his ancestors of Lower Brittany, strengthened by the climate of Canada, had made his head so vigorous that when he was struck upon it he scarce felt it; and when anything was graven in it, nothing could efface it. Nothing had ever escaped his memory. His conception was the more sure and lively, because his infancy had not been loaded with useless fooleries, which overwhelm ours. Things entered into his head without being clouded. The Prior at length resolved to make him read the New Testament. The Huron devoured it with great pleasure; but not knowing at what time, or in what country all the adventures related in this book had happened, he did not in the least doubt that the scene of action had been in Lower Brittany; and he swore, that he would cut off Caiphas and Pontius Pilate's ears, if ever he met those scoundrels.

His uncle, charmed with this good disposition, soon brought him to the point. He applauded his zeal, but at the same time acquainted him that it was needless, as these people had been dead upwards of 1690 years. The Huron soon got the whole book by heart. He sometimes proposed difficulties that greatly embarrassed the Prior. He was often obliged to consult the Abbé St. Yves, who, not knowing what to answer, brought a cleric of Lower Brittany to perfect the conversion of the Huron.

Grace, at length, operated; and the Huron promised to become a Christian. He did not doubt but that the first step toward it was circumcision.

"For," said he, "I do not find in the book that was put into my hands a single person who was not circumcised. It is therefore evident, that I must make a sacrifice to the Hebrew custom, and the sooner the better."

He sent for the surgeon of the village, and desired him to perform the operation. The surgeon, who had never performed such an operation, acquainted the family, who screamed out. The good Miss Kerkabon trembled lest her nephew, whom she knew to be resolute and expeditious, should perform the operation unskillfully himself; and that fatal consequences might ensue.

The Prior rectified the Huron's mistake, representing to him, that circumcision was no longer in fashion; that baptism was much more gentle and salutary; that the law of grace was not like the law of rigor. The Huron, who had much good sense, and was well disposed, disputed, but soon acknowledged his error, which seldom happens in Europe among disputants. In a word, he promised to let himself be baptized whenever they pleased.

The Bishop of St. Malo was chosen for the ceremony, who flattered, as may be believed, at baptizing a Huron, arrived in a pompous equipage, followed by his clergy. Miss St. Yves put on her best gown to bless God, and sent for a hairdresser from St. Malo's, to shine at the ceremony. The inquisitive bailiff brought the whole country with him. The church was magnificently ornamented. But when the Huron was summoned to attend the baptismal font, he was not to be found.

His uncle and aunt sought for him everywhere. It was imagined that he had gone a hunting, according to his usual custom. Everyone present at the festival, searched the neighboring woods and villages; but no intelligence could be obtained of the Huron. They began to fear he had returned to England. Some remembered that he had said he was very fond of that country. The Prior and his sister were persuaded that nobody was baptized there, and were troubled for their nephew's soul. The bishop was confounded, and ready to return home. The Prior and the Abbé St. Yves were in despair. The bailiff interrogated all passengers with his usual gravity. Miss Kerkabon melted into tears. Miss St. Yves did not weep, but she vented such deep sighs, as seemed to testify her sacramental disposition. They were walking in this melancholy mood, among the willows and reeds upon the banks of the little river Rence, when they perceived, in the middle of the stream, a large figure, tolerably white, with its two arms across its breast. They screamed out, and ran away. But curiosity being stronger than any other consideration, they advanced softly amongst the reeds; and when they were pretty certain they could not be seen, they were willing to descry what it was.

CHAPTER IV

The Huron Baptized

The Prior and the Abbé having run to the river side, they asked the Huron what he was doing?

"In faith," said he, "gentlemen, I am waiting to be baptized. I have been an hour in the water, up to my neck, and I do not think it is civil to let me be quite exhausted."

"My dear nephew," said the Prior to him, tenderly, "this is not the way of being baptized in Lower Brittany. Put on your clothes, and come with us."

Miss St. Yves, listening to the discourse, said in a whisper to her companion:

"Miss, do you think he will put his clothes on in such a hurry?"

The Huron, however, replied to the Prior:

"You will not make me believe now as you did before. I have studied very well since, and I am very certain there is no other kind of baptism. The eunuch of Queen Candace was baptized in a rivulet. I defy you to show me, in the book you gave me, that people were ever baptized in any other way. I either will not be baptized at all, or the ceremony shall be performed in the river."

It was in vain to remonstrate to him that customs were altered. He always recurred to the eunuch of Queen Candace. And though Miss and his aunt, who had observed him through the willows, were authorized to tell him, that he had no right to quote such a man; they, nevertheless, said nothing;—so great was their discretion.

The bishop came himself to speak to him, which was a great thing; but he could not prevail. The Huron disputed with the bishop.

"Show me," said he, "in the book my uncle gave me, one single man that was not baptized in a river, and I will do whatever you please."

His aunt, in despair, had observed, that the first time her nephew bowed, he made a much lower bow to Miss St. Yves, than to anyone in the company—that he had not even saluted the bishop with so much respect, blended with cordiality, as he did that agreeable young lady. She thought it advisable to apply to her in this great embarrassment. She earnestly entreated her to use her influence to engage the Huron to be baptized according to the custom of Brittany, thinking that her nephew could never be a Christian if he persisted in being christened in the stream.

Miss St. Yves blushed at the secret joy she felt in being appointed to execute so important a commission. She modestly approached the Huron, and squeezing his hand in quite a noble manner, she said to him:

"What, will you do nothing to please me?"

And in uttering these words, she raised her eyes from a downcast look into a graceful tenderness.

"O! yes, Miss, everything you require, all that you command, whether it is to be baptized in water, fire, or blood;—there is nothing I can refuse you."

Miss St. Yves had the glory of effecting, in two words, what neither the importunities of the Prior, the repeated interrogations of the bailiff, nor the reasoning of the bishop, could effect. She was sensible of her triumph; but she was not yet sensible of its utmost latitude.

Baptism was administered, and received with all the decency, magnificence, and propriety possible. His uncle and aunt yielded to the Abbé St. Yves and his sister the favor of supporting the Huron upon the font. Miss St. Yves's eyes sparkled with joy at being a godmother. She was ignorant how much this high title compromised her. She accepted the honor, without being acquainted with its fatal consequences.

As there never was any ceremony that was not followed by a good dinner, the company took their seats at table after the christening. The humorists of Lower Brittany said, "they did not choose to have their wine baptized." The Prior said, that wine, according to Solomon, cherished the heart of man." The bishop added, "that the Patriarch Judah ought to have tied his ass-colt to the vine, and steeped his cloak in the blood of the grape; and that he was sorry the same could not be done in Lower Brittany, to which God had not allotted vines." Everyone endeavored to say a good thing upon the Huron's christening, and strokes of gallantry to the godmother. The bailiff, ever interrogating, asked the Huron, if he was faithful in keeping his promises?"

"How," said he, "can I fail keeping them, since I have deposited them in the hands of Miss St. Yves?"

The Huron grew warm; he had drank repeatedly his godmother's health.

"If," said he, "I had been baptized with your hand, I feel that the water which was poured on the nape of my neck would have burnt me."

The bailiff thought that this was too poetical, being ignorant that allegory is a familiar figure in Canada. But his godmother was very well pleased.

The Huron had, at his baptism, received the name of Hercules.

CHAPTER V

The Huron in Love

It must be acknowledged, that from the time of this christening and this dinner, Miss St. Yves passionately wished that the bishop would again make her an assistant with Mr. Hercules in some other fine ceremony—that is, the marriage ceremony. However, as she was well brought up, and very modest,—she did not entirely agree with herself in regard to these tender sentiments; but if a look, a word, a gesture, a thought, escaped from her, she concealed it admirably under the veil of modesty. She was tender, lively, and sagacious.

As soon as the bishop was gone, the Huron and Miss St. Yves met together, without thinking they were in search of one another. They spoke together, without premeditating what they said. The sincere youth immediately declared, "that he loved her with all his heart; and that the beauteous Abacaba, with whom he had been desperately in love in his own country, was far inferior to her." Miss replied, with her usual modesty, "that the Prior, her uncle, and the lady, her aunt, should be spoken to immediately; and that, on her side, she would say a few words to her dear brother, the Abbé of St. Yves, and that she flattered herself it would meet with no opposition."

The youth replied: "that the consent of anyone was entirely superfluous that it appeared to him extremely ridiculous to go and ask others what they were to do; that when two parties were agreed, there was no occasion for a third, to accomplish their union."

"I never consult anyone," said he, "when I have a mind to breakfast, to hunt, or to sleep. I am sensible, that in love it is not amiss to have the consent of the person whom we wish for; but as I am neither in love with my uncle nor my aunt, I have no occasion to address myself to them in this affair; and if you will believe me, you may equally dispense with the advice of the Abbé of St. Yves."

It may be supposed that the young lady exerted all the delicacy of her wit, to bring her Huron to the terms of good breeding. She was very angry, but soon softened. In a word, it cannot be said how this conversation would have ended, if the declining day had not brought the Abbé to conduct his sister home. The Huron left his uncle and aunt to rest, they being somewhat fatigued with the ceremony, and long dinner. He passed part of the night in writing verses in the Huron language, upon his well-beloved; for it should be known, that there is no country where love has not rendered lovers poets.

The next day his uncle spoke to him in the following manner. "I am somewhat advanced in years. My brother has left only a little bit of ground, which is a very small matter. I have a good priory. If you will only make yourself a sub-deacon, as I hope you will, I will resign my priory in your favor; and you will live quite at your ease, after having been the consolation of my old age."

The Huron replied:

"Uncle, much good may it do you; live as long as you can. I do not know what it is to be a sub-deacon, or what it is to resign; but everything will be agreeable to me, provided I have Miss St. Yves at my disposal."

"Good heavens, nephew! what is it you say? Do you love that beautiful young lady so earnestly?"

"Yes, uncle."

"Alas! nephew, it is impossible you should ever marry her."

"It is very possible, uncle; for she did not only squeeze my hand when she left me, but she promised she would ask me in marriage. I certainly shall wed her."

"It is impossible, I tell you, she is your godmother. It is a dreadful sin for a godmother to give her hand to her godson. It is contrary to all laws, human and divine."

"Why the deuce, uncle, should it be forbidden to marry one's godmother, when she is young and handsome? I did not find, in the book you gave me, that it was wrong to marry young women who assisted at christenings. I perceive, every day, that an infinite number of things are done here which are not in your book, and nothing is done that is said in it. I must acknowledge to you, that this astonishes and displeases me. If I am deprived of the charming Miss St. Yves on account of my baptism, I give you notice, that I will run away with her and unbaptize myself."

The Prior was confounded; his sister wept.

Whilst he was yet speaking, the bailiff entered, and, according to his usual custom, asked him where he was going?

"I am going to get married," replied the ingenuous Hercules, running along; and in less than a quarter of an hour he was with his charming dear mistress, who was still asleep.

"Ah! my dear brother," said Miss Kerkabon to the Prior, "you will never make a sub-deacon of our nephew."

The bailiff was very much displeased at this journey; for he laid claim to Miss St. Yves in favor of his son, who was a still greater and more insupportable fool than his father.

CHAPTER VI

The Huron Flies to His Mistress, and Becomes Quite Furious

No sooner had the ingenuous Hercules reached the house, than having asked the old servant, which was his mistress's apartment, he forced open the door, which was badly fastened, and flew toward the bed. Miss St. Yves, startled out of her sleep, cried:

"Ah! what, is it you! Stop, what are you about?" He answered:

"I am going to marry."

She opposed him with all the decency of a young lady so well educated; but the Huron did not understand raillery, and found all evasions extremely disagreeable.

"Miss Abacaba, my first mistress," said he, "did not behave in this manner; you have no honesty; you promised me marriage, and you will not marry; this is being deficient in the first laws of honor."

The outcries of the lady, brought the sagacious Abbé de St. Yves with his housekeeper, an old devotee servant, and the parish priest. The sight of these moderated the courage of the assailant.

"Good heavens!" cried the Abbé, "my dear neighbor, what are you about?"

"My duty," replied the young man, "I am fulfilling my promises, which are sacred."

Miss St. Yves adjusted herself, not without blushing. The lover was conducted into another apartment. The Abbé remonstrated to him on the enormity of his conduct. The Huron defended himself upon the privileges of the law of nature, which he understood perfectly well. The Abbé maintained, that the law positive should be allowed all its advantages; and that without conventions agreed on between men, the law of nature must almost constantly be nothing more than natural felony.

The ingenuous Hercules made answer with the observation constantly adopted by savages:

"You are then very great rogues, since so many precautions are necessary."

This remark somewhat disconcerted the Abbé.

"There are, I acknowledge, libertines and cheats among us, and there would be as many among the Hurons, if they were united in a great city: but, at the same time, we have discreet, honest, enlightened people; and these are the men who have framed the laws. The more upright we are, the more readily we should submit to them, as we thereby set an example to the vicious, who respect those bounds which virtue has given herself."

This answer struck the Huron. It has already been observed, that his mind was well disposed. He was softened by flattering speeches, which promised him hopes; all the world is caught in these snares; and Miss St. Yves herself appeared, after having been at her toilet. Every thing was now conducted with the utmost good breeding.

It was with much difficulty that Hercules was sent back to his relations. It was again necessary for the charming Miss St. Yves to interfere; the more she perceived the influence she had upon him, the more she loved him. She made him depart, and was much affected at it. At length, when he was gone, the Abbé, who was not only Miss St. Yves's elder brother by many years, but was also her guardian, endeavored to wean his ward from the importunities of this dreadful lover. He went to consult the bailiff, who had always intended his son for the Abbé's sister, and who advised him to place the poor girl in a convent. This was a terrible stroke. Such a measure would, to a young lady unaffected with any particular passion, have been inexpressible punishment; but to a love-sick maid, equally sagacious and tender, it was despair itself.

When the ingenuous Hercules returned to the Prior's, he related all that had happened with his usual frankness. He met with the same remonstrances, which had some effect upon his mind, though none upon his senses; but the next day, when he wanted to return to his mistress, in order to reason with her upon the law of nature and the law of convention, the bailiff acquainted him, with insulting joy, that she was in a convent.

"Very well," said he, "I'll go and reason with her in this convent."

"That cannot be," said the bailiff; and then entered into a long explanation of the nature of a convent, telling him that this word was derived from *conventus,* in the Latin, which signifies "an assembly"; and the Huron could not comprehend, why he might not be admitted into this assembly; he became as furious as was his patron Hercules, when Euritus, king of Oechalia, no less cruel than the Abbé of St. Yves, refused him the beauteous Iola, his daughter, not inferior in beauty to the Abbé's sister. He was upon the point of going to set fire to the convent to carry off his mistress, or be burnt with her. Miss Kerkabon, terrified at such a declaration, gave up all hopes of ever seeing her nephew a sub-deacon; and, sadly weeping, she exclaimed: "The devil has certainly been in him since he has been christened."

CHAPTER VII

The Huron Repulses the English

THE INGENUOUS HERCULES WALKED TOWARD THE SEA-COAST, wrapped in deep and gloomy melancholy, with his double-charged fusee upon his shoulder, and his cutlass by his side, shooting now and then a bird, and often tempted to shoot himself; but he had still some affection for life, for the sake of his dear mistress; by turns execrating his uncle and aunt, all Lower Brittany, and his christening; then blessing them, as they had introduced him to the knowledge of her he loved. He resolved upon going to burn the convent, and he stopped short for fear of burning his mistress. The waves of the Channel are not more agitated by the easterly and westerly winds, than was his heart by so many contrary emotions.

He was walking along very fast, without knowing whither he was going, when he heard the beat of a drum. He saw, at a great distance, a vast multitude, part of whom ran toward the coast, and the other part in the opposite direction.

A thousand shrieks re-echoed on every side. Curiosity and courage hurried him, that instant, toward the spot where the greatest clamor arose, which he attained in a few leaps. The commander of the militia, who had supped with him at the Prior's, knew him immediately, and he ran to the Huron with open arms:

"Ah! it is the sincere American: he will fight for us."

Upon which the militia, who were almost dead with fear, recovered themselves, crying with one voice:

"It is the Huron, the ingenuous Huron."

"Gentlemen," said he, "what is the matter? Why are you frightened? Have they shut your mistresses up in convents?"

Instantly a thousand confused voices cried out:

"Do you not see the English, who are landing?"

"Very well," replied the Huron, "they are a brave people; they never proposed making me a sub-deacon; they never carried off my mistress."

The commander made him understand, that they were coming to pillage the Abbé of the Mountain, drink his uncle's wine, and perhaps carry off Miss St. Yves; that the little vessel which set him on shore in Brittany had come only to reconnoitre the coast; that they were committing acts of hostility, without having declared war against France; and that the province was entirely exposed to them.

"If this be the case," said he, "they violate the law of nature: let me alone; I lived a long time among them; I am acquainted with their language, and I will speak to them. I cannot think they can have so wicked a design."

During this conversation the English fleet had approached; the Huron ran toward it, and having jumped into a little boat, soon rowed to the Admiral's ship, and having gone on board, asked "whether it was true, that they were come to ravage the coast, without having honestly declared war?"

The Admiral and his crew burst out into laughter, made him drink some punch, and sent him back.

The ingenuous Hercules, piqued at this reception, thought of nothing else but beating his old friends for his countrymen and the Prior. The gentlemen of the neighborhood ran from all quarters, and joined them: they had some cannon, and he discharged them one after the other. The English landed, and he flew toward them, when he killed three of them with his own hand. He even wounded the Admiral, who had made a joke of him. The entire militia were animated with his prowess. The English returned to their ships, and went on board; and the whole coast re-echoed with the shouts of victory, "Live the king! live the ingenuous Hercules!"

Everyone ran to embrace him; everyone strove to stop the bleeding of some slight wounds he had received.

"Ah!" said he, "if Miss St. Yves were here, she would put on a plaster for me."

The bailiff who had hid himself in his cellar during the battle, came to pay his compliments like the rest. But he was greatly surprised, when he heard the ingenuous Hercules say to a dozen young men, well disposed for his service, who surrounded him:

"My friends, having delivered the Abbé of the Mountain is nothing; we must rescue a nymph."

The warm blood of these youths was fired at the expression. He was already followed by crowds, who repaired to the convent. If the bailiff had not immediately acquainted the commandant with their design, and he had not sent a detachment after the joyous troop, the thing would have been done. The Huron was conducted back to his uncle and aunt, who overwhelmed him with tears and tenderness.

"I see very well," said his uncle, "that you will never be either a sub-deacon or a prior; you will be an officer, and one still braver than my brother the Captain, and probably as poor."

Miss Kerkabon could not stop an incessant flow of tears, whilst she embraced him, saying, "he will be killed too, like my brother; it were much better he were a sub-deacon."

The Huron had, during the battle, picked up a purse full of guineas, which the Admiral had probably lost. He did not doubt but that this purse would buy all Lower Brittany, and, above all, make Miss St. Yves a great lady. Everyone persuaded him to repair to Versailles, to receive the recompense due to his services. The commandant, and the principal officers, furnished him with certificates in abundance. The uncle and aunt also approved of this journey. He was to be presented to the king without any difficulty. This alone would give him great weight in the province. These two good folks added to the English purse a considerable present out of their savings. The Huron said to himself, "When I see the king, I will ask Miss St. Yves of him in marriage, and certainly he will not refuse me." He set out accordingly, amidst the acclamations of the whole district, stifled with embraces, bathed in tears by his aunt, blessed by his uncle, and recommending himself to the charming Miss St. Yves.

CHAPTER VIII

The Huron Goes to Court. Sups Upon the Road with Some Huguenots.

THE INGENUOUS HERCULES TOOK THE SAUMUR ROAD IN THE coach, because there was at that time no other convenience. When he came to Saumur, he was astonished to find the city almost deserted, and to see several families going away. He was told, that half a dozen years before, Saumur contained upwards of fifty thousand inhabitants, and that at present there were not six thousand. He mentioned this at the inn, whilst at supper. Several Protestants were at table; some complained bitterly, others trembled with rage, others, weeping, said, *Nos dulcia linquimus arva, nos patriam fugimus.* The Huron, who did not understand Latin, had these words explained to him, which signified, "We abandon our sweet fields;—We fly from our country."

"And why do you fly from your country, gentlemen?"

"Because we must otherwise acknowledge the Pope."

"And why not acknowledge him? You have no godmothers, then, that you want to marry; for, I am told it is he that grants this permission."

"Ah! sir, this Pope says, that he is master of the domains of kings."

"But, gentlemen, what religion are you of?"

"Why, sir, we are for the most part drapers and manufacturers."

"If the Pope, then, is not the master of your clothes and manufactures, you do very well not to acknowledge him; but as to kings, it is their business, and why do you trouble yourselves about it?"

Here a little black man took up the argument, and very learnedly set forth the grievances of the company. He talked of the revocation of the edict of Nantes with so much energy; he deplored, in so pathetic a manner, the fate of fifty thousand fugitive families, and of fifty thousand others converted by dragoons; that the ingenuous Hercules could not refrain from shedding tears.

"Whence arises it," said he, "that so great a king, whose renown expands itself even to the Hurons, should thus deprive himself of so many hearts that would have loved him, and so many arms that would have served him."

"Because he has been imposed upon, like other great kings," replied the little orator, "He has been made to believe, that as soon as he utters a word, all people think as he does; and that he can make us change our religion, just as his musician Lulli, in a moment, changes the decorations of his opera. He has not only already lost five or six hundred thousand very useful subjects, but he has turned many of them into enemies; and King William, who is at this time master of England, has formed several regiments of these identical Frenchmen, who would otherwise have fought for their monarch."

"Such a disaster is more astonishing, as the present Pope, to whom Louis XIV sacrifices a part of his people, is his declared enemy. A violent quarrel has subsisted between them for nearly nine years. It has been carried so far, that France was in hopes of at length casting off the yoke, by which it has been kept in subjection for so many ages to this foreigner, and, more particularly, of not giving him any more money, which is the *primum mobile* of the affairs of this world. It, therefore, appears evident, that this great king has been imposed on, as well with respect to his interest, as the extent of his power, and that even the magnanimity of his heart has been struck at."

The Huron, becoming more and more interested, asked: "Who were the Frenchmen who thus deceived a monarch so dear to the Hurons?"

"They are the clerics," he was answered, "and, particularly, the king's adviser. It is to be hoped that God will one day punish them for it, and that they will be driven out, as they now drive us. Can any misfortune equal ours? Mons. de Louvois besets us on all sides with clerics and dragoons."

"Well, gentlemen," replied the Huron, "I am going to Versailles to receive the recompense due to my services; I will speak to Mons. de Louvois. I am told it is he who makes war from his closet. I shall see the king, and I will acquaint him with the truth. It is impossible not to yield to this truth, when it is felt. I shall return very soon to marry Miss St. Yves, and I beg you will be present at our nuptials."

These good people now took him for some great Lord, who travelled *incognito* in the coach. Some took him for the king's fool.

There was at table a disguised cleric, who acted as a spy to the king's adviser. He gave him an account of everything that passed, and he reported it to M. de Louvois. The spy wrote. The Huron and the letter arrived almost at the same time at Versailles.

CHAPTER IX

The Arrival of the Huron at Versailles. His Reception at Court.

THE INGENUOUS HERCULES WAS SET DOWN FROM A PUBLIC CARriage, in the court of the kitchens. He asks the chairmen, what hour the king can be seen? The chairmen laugh in his face, just as the English Admiral had done: and he treated them in the same manner—he beat them. They were for retaliation, and the scene had like to have proved bloody, if a soldier, who was a gentleman of Brittany, had not passed by, and who dispersed the mob.

"Sir," said the traveler to him, "you appear to me to be a brave man. I am nephew to the Prior of Our Lady of the Mountain. I have killed Englishmen, and I am come to speak to the king: I beg you will conduct me to his chamber."

The soldier, delighted to find a man of courage from his province, who did not seem acquainted with the customs of the court, told him it was necessary to be presented to M. de Louvois.

"Very well, then, conduct me to M. de Louvois, who will doubtless conduct me to the king."

"It is more difficult to speak to M. de Louvois than the king. But I will conduct you to Mr. Alexander, first commissioner of war, and this will be just the same as if you spoke to the minister."

They accordingly repair to Mr. Alexander's, who is first clerk; but they cannot be introduced, he being closely engaged in business with a lady of the court, and no person is allowed admittance.

"Well," said the soldier, "there is no harm done, let us go to Mr. Alexander's first clerk. This will be just the same as if you spoke to Mr. Alexander himself."

The Huron quite astonished, followed him. They remained together half an hour in a little ante-chamber.

"What is all this?" said the ingenuous Hercules. "Is all the world invisible in this country? It is much easier to fight in Lower Brittany against Englishmen, than to meet with people at Versailles, with whom one hath business."

He amused himself for some time with relating his amours to his countryman; but the clock striking, recalled the soldier to his post, when a mutual promise was given of meeting on the morrow.

The Huron remained another half hour in the ante-chamber, meditating upon Miss St. Yves, and the difficulty of speaking to kings and first clerks.

At length the patron appeared.

"Sir," said the ingenuous Hercules, "If I had waited to repulse the English as long as you have made me wait for my audience, they would certainly have ravaged all Lower Brittany without opposition."

These words impressed the clerk. He at length said to the inhabitant of Brittany, "What is your request?"

"A recompense," said the other: "these are my titles"; showing his certificates.

The clerk read, and told him, "that probably he might obtain leave to purchase a lieutenancy."

"Me? what, must I pay money for having repulsed the English? Must I pay a tax to be killed for you, whilst you are peaceably giving your audience here? You are certainly jesting. I require a company of cavalry for nothing. I require that the king shall set Miss St. Yves at liberty from the convent, and give her to me in marriage. I want to speak to the king in favor of fifty thousand families, whom I propose restoring to him. In a word, I want to be useful. Let me be employed and advanced."

"What is your name, sir, who talk in such a high style?"

"Oh! oh!" answered the Huron; "you have not then read my certificates? This is the way they are treated. My name is *Hercules de Kerkabon.* I am christened, and I lodge at the Blue Dial." The clerk concluded, like the people at Saumur, that his head was turned, and did not pay him any further attention.

The same day, the king's adviser received his spy's letter, which accused the Breton Kerkabon of favoring in his heart the Huguenots, and condemning the conduct of the clerics. M. de Louvois had, on his side, received a letter from the inquisitive bailiff, which depicted the Huron as a wicked, lewd fellow, inclined to burn convents.

Hercules, after having walked in the gardens of Versailles, which had become irksome to him; after having supped like a native of Huronia and Lower Brittany: had gone to rest, in the pleasant hope of seeing the king the next day; of obtaining Miss St. Yves in marriage; of having, at least, a company of cavalry; and of setting aside the persecution against the Huguenots. He was rocking himself asleep with these flattering ideas, when the *Marechaussée* entered his chamber, and seized upon his double-charged fusee and his great sabre.

They took an inventory of his ready money, and then conducted him to the castle erected by King Charles V, son to John II, near the street of St. Antoine, at the gates des Tournelles.

What was the Huron's astonishment on his way thither the reader is left to imagine. He at first fancied it was all a dream; and remained for some time in a state of stupefaction. Presently, transported with rage, that gave him more than common strength, he collared two of his conductors who were with him in the coach, flung them out of the door, cast himself after them, and then dragged the third, who wanted to hold him. He fell in the attempt, when they tied him, and replaced him in the carriage.

"This, then," said he, "is what one gets for driving the English out of Lower Brittany! What wouldst thou say, charming Miss St. Yves, if thou didst see me in this situation?"

They at length arrived at the place of their destination. He was carried without any noise into the chamber in which he was to be locked up, like a dead corpse going to the grave. This room was already occupied by an old solitary student of Port Royal, named Gordon, who had been languishing here for two years.

"See," said the chief of the Marechaussée, "here is company I bring you"; and immediately the enormous bolts of this strong door, secured with large iron bars, were fastened upon them. These two captives were thus separated from all the universe besides.

CHAPTER X

The Huron Is Shut Up in the Bastille with a Jansenist

Mr. Gordon was a healthy old man, of a serene disposition, who was acquainted with two great things; the one was, to bear adversity; the other, to console the afflicted. He approached his companion with an open sympathizing air, and said to him, whilst he embraced him:

"Whoever thou art that is come to partake of my grave, be assured, that I shall constantly forget myself to soften thy torments in the infernal abyss where we are plunged. Let us adore Providence that has conducted us here. Let us suffer in peace, and trust in hope."

These words had the same effect upon the youth as cordial drops, which recall a dying person to life, and show to his astonished eyes a glimpse of light.

After the first compliments were over, Gordon, without urging him to relate the cause of his misfortune, inspired him by the sweetness of his discourse and by that interest which two unfortunate persons share with each other, with a desire of opening his heart and of disburdening himself of the weight which oppressed him; but he could not guess the cause of his misfortune, and the good man Gordon was as much astonished as himself.

"God must, doubtless," said the Jansenist to the Huron, "have great designs upon you, since he conducted you from Lake

Ontario into England, from thence to France; caused you to be baptized in Lower Brittany, and has now lodged you here for your salvation."

"I' faith," replied Hercules, "I believe the devil alone has interfered in my destiny. My countrymen in America would never have treated me with the barbarity that I have here experienced; they have not the least idea of it. They are called savages;—they are good people, but rustic; and the men of this country are refined villains. I am indeed, greatly surprised to have come from another world, to be shut up in this, under four bolts with a cleric; but I consider what an infinite number of men set out from one hemisphere to go and get killed in the other, or are cast away in the voyage, and are eaten by the fishes. I cannot discover the gracious designs of God over all these people."

Their dinner was brought them through a wicket. The conversation turned upon Providence, *lettres de cachet,* and upon the art of not sinking under disgrace, to which all men in this world are exposed.

"It is now two years since I have been here," said the old man, "without any other consolation than myself and books; and yet I have never been a single moment out of temper."

"Ah! Mr. Gordon," cried Hercules, "you are not then in love with your godmother. If you were as well acquainted with Miss St. Yves as I am, you would be in a state of desperation."

At these words he could not refrain from tears, which greatly relieved him from his oppression.

"How is it then that tears solace us?" said the Huron. "It seems to me that they should have quite an opposite effect."

"My son," said the good old man, "every thing is physical about us; all secretions are useful to the body, and all that comforts it, comforts the soul. We are the machines of Providence."

The ingenuous Huron, who, as we have already observed more than once, had a great share of understanding, entered deeply into the consideration of this idea, the seeds whereof appeared to be in himself. After which he asked his companion:

"Why his machine had for two years been confined by four bolts?"

"By effectual grace," answered Gordon; "I pass for a Jansenist; I know Arnaud and Nicole; the clerics have persecuted us."

"This is very strange," said the Huron, "all the unhappy people I have met with have been made so solely by persecution. With respect to your effectual grace, I acknowledge I do not understand what you mean. But I consider it as a very great favor, that God has let me, in my misfortunes, meet with a man, who pours into my heart such consolation as I thought myself incapable of receiving."

The conversation became each day more interesting and instructive. The souls of the two captives seemed to unite in one body. The old man had acquired knowledge, and the young man was willing to receive instruction. At the end of the first month, he eagerly applied himself to the study of geometry. Gordon made him read *Rohault's Physics*, which book was still in fashion; and he had good sense enough to find in it nothing but doubts and uncertainties.

He afterward read the first volume of the *Enquiry After Truth*. This instructive work gave him new light.

"What!" said he, "do our imagination and our senses deceive us to that degree? What, are not our ideas formed by objects, and can we not acquire them by ourselves?"

When he had gone through the second volume, he was not so well satisfied; and he concluded it was much easier to destroy than to build.

His colleague, astonished that a young ignoramus should make such a remark, conceived a very high opinion of his understanding, and was more strongly attached to him.

"Your Malebranche," said he to Gordon one day, "seems to have written half his book whilst he was in possession of his reason, and the other half with the assistance only of imagination and prejudice."

Some days after, Gordon asked him what he thought of the soul, and the manner in which we receive our ideas of volition, grace, and free agency.

"Nothing," replied the Huron. "If I think sometimes, it is that we are under the power of the Eternal Being, like the stars and the elements—that he operates everything in us—that we are small wheels of the immense machine, of which he is the soul—that he acts according to general laws, and not from particular views. This is all that appears to me intelligible; all the rest is to me a dark abyss."

"But this, my son, would be making God the author of sin!"

"But, father, your effectual grace would equally make him the author of sin; for certainly all those to whom this grace was refused, would sin; and is not an all-powerful being who permits evil, virtually the author of evil?"

This sincerity greatly embarrassed the good man; he found that all his endeavors to extricate himself from this quagmire were ineffectual; and he heaped such quantities of words upon one another, which seemed to have meaning, but which in fact had none, that the Huron could not help pitying him. This question evidently determined the origin of good and evil; and poor Gordon was reduced to the necessity of recurring to Pandora's box—Oromasdes's egg pierced by Arimanes—the enmity between Typhon and Osiris—and, at last, original sin; and these he huddled together in profound darkness, without their throwing the least glimmering light upon one another. However, this romance of the soul diverted their thoughts from the contemplation of their own misery; and, by a strange magic, the multitude of calamities dispersed throughout the world diminished the sensation of their own miseries. They did not dare complain when all mankind was in a state of sufferance.

But in the repose of night, the image of the charming Miss St. Yves effaced from the mind of her lover every metaphysical and moral idea. He awoke with his eyes bathed in tears; and the old Jansenist forgot his effectual grace, and the Abbé of St. Cyran, and even Jansenius himself, to afford consolation to a youth whom he had judged guilty of a mortal sin.

After these lectures and their reasonings were over, their adventures furnished them with subjects of conversation; after this store was exhausted, they read together, or separately. The Huron's understanding daily increased; and he would certainly have made great progress in mathematics, if the thought of Miss St. Yves had not frequently distracted him.

He read histories, which made him melancholy. The world appeared to him too wicked and too miserable. In fact, history is nothing more than a picture of crimes and misfortunes. The crowd of innocent and peaceable men are always invisible upon this vast theatre. The *dramatis personae* are composed of ambitious, perverse men. The pleasure which history affords is derived from the same source as tragedy, which would languish and become insipid, were it not inspired with strong passions, great events, and piteous misfortunes. Clio must be armed with a poniard as well as Melpomene.

Though the history of France is not less filled with horror than those of other nations, it nevertheless appeared to him so disgusting in the beginning, so dry in the continuation, and so trifling in the end, (even in the time of Henry IV); ever destitute of grand monuments, or foreign to those fine discoveries which have illustrated other nations; that he was obliged to resolve upon not being tired, in order to go through all the particulars of obscure calamities confined to a little corner of the world.

Gordon thought like him. They both laughed with pity when they read of the sovereigns of Fezensacs, Fesansaguet, and Astrac: such a study could be relished only by their heirs, if they had any. The brilliant ages of the Roman Republic made him sometimes quite indifferent as to any other part of the globe. The spectacle of victorious Rome, the lawgiver of nations, engrossed his whole soul. He glowed in contemplating a people who were governed for seven hundred years by the enthusiasm of liberty and glory.

Thus rolled days, weeks, and months; and he would have thought himself happy in the sanctuary of despair, if he had not loved.

The natural goodness of his heart was softened still more when he reflected upon the Prior of Our Lady of the Mountain, and the sensible Kerkabon.

"What must they think," he would often repeat, "when they can get no tidings of me? They must think me an ungrateful wretch." This idea rendered him inconsolable. He pitied those who loved him much more than he pitied himself.

CHAPTER XI

How the Huron Discloses His Genius

Reading aggrandizes the soul, and an enlightened friend affords consolation. Our captive had these two advantages in his favor which he had never expected.

"I shall begin to believe in the Metamorphoses," said he, "for I have been transformed from a brute into a man."

He formed a chosen library with part of the money which he was allowed to dispose of. His friend encouraged him to commit to writing such observations as occurred to him. These are his notes upon ancient history:

"I imagine that nations were for a long time like myself; that they did not become enlightened till very late; that for many ages they were occupied with nothing but the present moment which elapsed: that they thought very little of what was past, and never of the future. I have traversed five or six hundred leagues in Canada, and I did not meet with a single monument: no one is the least acquainted with the actions of his predecessors. Is not this the natural state of man? The human species of this continent appears to me superior to that of the other. They have extended their being for many ages by arts and knowledge. Is this because they have beards upon their chins and God has refused this ornament to the Americans? I do not believe it; for I find the Chinese have very little beard, and that they have cultivated arts for upwards of five thousand years. In effect, if their annals go back upwards of four thousand years, the nation must necessarily have been united and in a flourishing state more than five hundred centuries.

"One thing particularly strikes me in this ancient history of China, which is, that almost every thing is probable and natural. I admire it because it is not tinctured with anything of the marvelous.

"Why have all other nations adopted fabulous origins? The ancient chronicles of the history of France, which, by the by, are not very ancient, make the French descend from one Francus, the son of Hector. The Romans said they were the issue of a Phrygian, though there was not in their whole language a single word that had the least connection with the language of Phrygia. The gods had inhabited Egypt for ten thousand years, and the devils Scythia, where they had engendered the Huns. I meet with nothing before Thucydides but romances similar to the Amadis, and far less amusing. Apparitions, oracles, prodigies, sorcery, metamorphoses, are interspersed throughout with the explanation of dreams, which are the bases of the destiny of the greatest empires and the smallest states. Here are speaking beasts, there brutes that are adored, gods transformed into men, and men into gods. If we must have fables, let us, at least, have such as appear the emblem of truth. I admire the fables of philosophers, but I laugh at those of children, and hate those of impostors."

He one day hit upon a history of the Emperor Justinian. It was there related, that some Appedeutes of Constantinople had delivered, in very bad Greek, an edict against the greatest captain of the age, because this hero had uttered the following words in the warmth of conversation: "Truth shines forth with its proper light, and people's minds are not illumined with flaming piles." The Appedeutes declared that this proposition was heretical, bordering upon heresy; and that the contrary action was catholic, universal, and Grecian: "The minds of the people are enlightened but with flaming piles, and truth cannot shine forth with its own light." These Linostolians thus condemned several discourses of the captain, and published an edict.

"What!" said the Huron, with much emotion, "shall such people publish edicts?"

"They are not edicts," replied Gordon: "they are contradictions, which all the world laughed at in Constantinople, and the Emperor the first. He was a wise prince, who knew how to reduce the Linostolian Appedeutes to a state incapable of doing anything but good. He knew that these gentlemen, and several other Pastophores, had tired the patience of the Emperors, his predecessors, with contradictions in more serious matters."

"He did quite right," said the Huron, "the Pastophores should not be supported, but constrained."

He committed several other observations to paper, which astonished old Gordon. "What," said he to himself, "have I consumed fifty years in instruction and not attained to the degree of natural good sense of this child, who is almost a savage? I tremble to think I have so arduously strengthened prejudices, and he listens to simple nature only."

The good man had some little books of criticism, some of those periodical pamphlets wherein men, incapable of producing anything themselves, blacken the productions of others; where a Vise insults a Racine, and a Faidit a Fenelon. The Huron ran over some of them. "I compare them," said he, "to certain gnats that lodge their eggs in the nostrils of the finest horses, which do not, however, retard their speed."

The two philosophers scarce deigned to cast their eyes upon these dregs of literature.

They soon after went through the elements of astronomy. The Huron sent for some globes: he was ravished at this great spectacle.

"How hard it is," said he, "that I should only begin to be acquainted with heaven, when the power of contemplating it is ravished from me! Jupiter and Saturn revolve in these immense spaces;—millions of suns illumine myriads of worlds; and, in this corner of the earth on which I am cast, there are beings that deprive me of seeing and studying those worlds to which my eye might reach, and even that in which God has placed me. The light created for the whole universe is lost to me. It was not hidden from me in the northern horizon, where I passed my infancy and youth. Without you, my dear Gordon, I should be annihilated."

CHAPTER XII

The Huron's Sentiments Upon Theatrical Pieces

THE YOUNG HURON RESEMBLED ONE OF THOSE VIGOROUS TREES, which, languishing in an ungrateful soil, extend in a little time their roots and branches when transplanted to a more favorable spot; and it was very extraordinary that this favorable spot should be a prison.

Among the books which employed the leisure of the two captives were some poems and also translations of Greek tragedies, and some dramatic pieces in French. Those passages that dwelt on love communicated at once pleasure and pain to the soul of the Huron. They were but so many images of his dear Miss St. Yves. The fable of the two pigeons rent his heart: for he was far estranged from his tender dove.

Molière enchanted him. He taught him the manners of Paris and of human nature.

"To which of his comedies do you give the preference?"

"Doubtless to his *Tartuffe*."

"I am of your opinion," said Gordon; "it was a Tartuffe that flung me into this dungeon, and perhaps they were Tartuffes who have been the cause of your misfortunes."

"What do you think of these Greek tragedies?"

"They are very good for Grecians."

But when he read the modern *Iphigenia, Phoedrus, Andromache,* and *Athalia*, he was in ecstasy, he sighed, he wept,—and he learned them by heart, without having any such intention.

"Read *Rodogune*," said Gordon; "that is said to be a capital production; the other pieces which have given you so much pleasure, are trifles compared to this."

The young man had scarce got through the first page, before he said, "This is not written by the same author."

"How do you know it?"

"I know nothing yet: but these lines neither touch my ear nor my heart."

"O!" said Gordon, "the versification does not signify." The Huron asked, "What must I judge by then?"

After having read the piece very attentively without any other design than being pleased, he looked steadfastly at his friend with much astonishment, not knowing what to say. At length, being urged to give his opinion with respect to what he felt, this was the answer he made: "I understood very little of the beginning; the middle disgusted me; but the last scene greatly moved me, though there appears to me but little probability in it. I have no prejudices for or against any one, but I do not remember twenty lines, I, who recollect them all when they please me."

"This piece, nevertheless, passes for the best upon our stage."

"If that be the case," said he, "it is perhaps like many people who are not worthy of the places they hold. After all, this is a matter of taste, and mine cannot yet be formed. I may be mistaken; but you know I am accustomed to say what I think or rather what I feel. I suspect that illusion, fashion, caprice, often warp the judgments of men."

Here he repeated some lines from *Iphigenia*, which he was full of; and though he declaimed but indifferently, he uttered them with such truth and emotion that he made the old Jansenist weep. He then read *Cinna*, which did not excite his tears, but his admiration.

CHAPTER XIII

The Beautiful Miss St. Yves Goes to Versailles

WHILST THE UNFORTUNATE HERCULES WAS MORE ENLIGHTENED than consoled; whilst his genius, so long stifled, unfolded itself with so much rapidity and strength; whilst nature, which was attaining a degree of perfection in him, avenged herself of the outrages of fortune; what became of the Prior, his good sister, and the beautiful recluse, Miss St. Yves? The first month they were uneasy, and the third they were immersed in sorrow. False conjectures, ill-grounded reports, alarmed them. At the end of six months, it was concluded he was dead. At length, Mr. and Miss Kerkabon learned, by a letter of ancient date, which one of the king's guards had written to Brittany, that a young man resembling the Huron arrived one night at Versailles, but that since that time no one had heard him spoken of.

"Alas," said Miss Kerkabon, "our nephew had done some ridiculous thing, which has brought on some terrible consequences. He is young, a *Low Breton*, and cannot know how to behave at court. My dear brother, I never saw Versailles nor Paris; here is a fine opportunity, and we shall perhaps find our poor nephew. He is our brother's son, and it is our duty to assist him. Who knows? we may perhaps at length prevail upon him to become a sub-deacon when the fire of youth is somewhat abated. He was much inclined to the sciences. Do you recollect how he reasoned upon the Old and New Testaments? We are answerable for his soul. He was baptized at our instigation. His dear mistress Miss St. Yves does nothing but weep incessantly. Indeed, we must go to Paris. If he is concealed in any of those infamous houses of pleasure, which I have often heard of, we will get him out."

The Prior was affected at his sister's discourse. He went in search of the Bishop of St. Malo's, who had baptized the Huron, and requested his protection and advice. The Prelate approved of the journey. He gave the Prior letters of recommendation to the king's adviser, who was invested with the first dignitary in the kingdom.

At length, the brother and sister set out; but when they came to Paris, they found themselves bewildered in a great labyrinth without clue or end. Their fortune was but middling, and they had occasion every day for carriages to pursue their discovery, which they could not accomplish.

He at length saw the minister, who received him with open arms, protesting he had always entertained the greatest private esteem for him, though he had never known him. He swore that his society had always been attached to the inhabitants of Lower Brittany.

"But," said he, "has not your nephew the misfortune of being a Huguenot?"

"No, certainly."

"May he not be a Jansenist?"

"I can assure you that he is scarce a Christian. It is about eleven months since he was christened."

"This is very well;—we will take care of him. Is your benefice considerable?"

"No, a very trifle, and our nephew costs us a great deal."

"Are there any Jansenists in your neighborhood? Take great care, my dear Mr. Prior, they are more dangerous than Huguenots, or even Atheists."

"We have none; it is not even known at Our Lady of the Mountain what Jansenism is."

"So much the better; go, there is nothing I will not do for you."

He dismissed the Prior in this affectionate manner, but thought no more about him.

Time slipped away, and the Prior and his good sister were almost in despair.

In the meanwhile, the cursed bailiff urged very strenuously the marriage of his great booby son with the beautiful Miss St. Yves, who was taken purposely out of the convent. She always entertained a passion for her godson in proportion as she detested the husband who was designed for her. The insult that had been offered her, by shutting her up in a convent, increased her affection; and the mandate for wedding the bailiff's son completed her antipathy for him. Chagrin, tenderness, and terror, racked her soul. Love, we know, is much more inventive and more daring in a young woman than friendship in an aged prior and an aunt upwards of forty-five. Besides, she had received good instructions in her convent with the assistance of romances, which she read by stealth.

The beautiful Miss St. Yves remembered the letter that had been sent by one of the king's guards to Lower Brittany, which had been spoken of in the province. She resolved to go herself and gain information at Versailles; to throw herself at the minister's feet, if her husband should be in prison as it was said, and obtain justice for him. I know not what secret intelligence she had gained that at court nothing is refused to a pretty woman; but she knew not the price of these boons.

Having taken this resolution, it afforded her some consolation; and she enjoyed some tranquillity without upbraiding Providence with the severity of her lot. She receives her detested intended father-in-law, caresses her brother, and spreads happiness throughout the house. On the day appointed for the ceremony, she secretly departs at four o'clock in the morning, with the little nuptial presents she has received, and all she could gather. Her plan was so well laid, that she was about ten leagues upon her journey, when, about noon, her absence was discovered, and when everyone's consternation and surprise was inexpressible. The inquisitive bailiff asked more questions that day than he had done for a week before; the intended bridegroom was more stupefied than ever. The Abbé St. Yves resolved in his rage to pursue his sister. The bailiff and his son were disposed to accompany him. Thus fate led almost the whole canton of Lower Brittany to Paris.

The beautiful Miss St. Yves was not without apprehensions that she should be pursued. She rode on horseback, and she got all the intelligence she could from the couriers, without being suspected. She asked if they had not met an abbé, an enormous bailiff, and a young booby, galloping as fast as they could to Paris. Having learned, on the third day, that they were not far behind, she took quite a different road, and was skillful and lucky enough to arrive at Versailles, whilst they were in a fruitless pursuit after her, at Paris. But how was she to behave at Versailles? Young, handsome, untutored, unsupported, unknown, exposed to every danger, how could she dare go in search of one of the king's guards? She had some thoughts of applying to a cleric of low rank, for there were some for every station of life; as God, they say, has given different aliments to every species of animals. The beautiful Miss St. Yves addressed herself to one of these last, who was called *Tout-a-tous* (all to everyone). She set forth her adventure, her situation, her danger, and conjured him to get her a lodging with some good devotee, who might shelter her from temptation.

Tout-a-tous introduced her to the wife of the cup-bearer, one of his most trusty friends. From the moment Miss St. Yves became her lodger, she did her utmost to obtain the confidence and friendship of this person. She gained intelligence of the Breton-Guard, and invited him to visit her. Having learned from him that her lover had been carried off after having had a conference with one of the clerks, she flew to this clerk. The sight of a fine woman softened him, for it must be allowed God created woman only to tame mankind.

The scribe, thus mollified, acknowledged to her everything.

"Your lover has been in the bastile almost a year, and without your intercession he would, perhaps, have ended his days there."

The tender Miss St. Yves swooned at this intelligence. When she had recovered herself, her informer told her:

"I have no power to do good; all my influence extends to doing harm. Take my advice, wait upon M. de St. Pouange, who has the power of doing both good and ill; he is Mons. de Louvois's cousin and favorite. This minister has two souls: the one is M. de St. Pouange, and Mademoiselle de Belle is the other, but she is at present absent from Versailles; so that you have nothing to do but captivate the protector I have pointed out to you."

The beautiful Miss St. Yves, divided between some trifling joy and excessive grief, between a glimmering of hope and dreadful apprehensions;—pursued by her brother, idolizing her lover, wiping her tears, which flowed in torrents; trembling and feeble, yet summoning all her courage;—in this situation, she flew on the wings of love to M. de St. Pouange's.

CHAPTER XIV

Rapid Progress of the Huron's Intellect

THE INGENUOUS YOUTH WAS MAKING A RAPID PROGRESS IN THE sciences, and particularly in the science of man. The cause of this sudden disclosure of his understanding was as much owing to his savage education as to the disposition of his soul; for, having learned nothing in his infancy, he had not imbibed any prejudices. His mind, not having been warped by error, had retained all its primitive rectitude. He saw things as they were; whereas the ideas that are communicated to us in our infancy make us see them all our life in a false light.

"Your persecutors are very abominable wretches," said he to his friend Gordon. "I pity you for being oppressed, but I condemn you for being a Jansenist. All sects appear to me to be founded in error. Tell me if there be any sectaries in geometry?"

"No, my child," said the good old Gordon, heaving a deep sigh; "all men are agreed concerning truth when demonstrated, but they are too much divided about latent truths."

"If there were but one single hidden truth in your load of arguments, which have been so often sifted for such a number of ages, it would doubtless have been discovered, and the universe would certainly have been unanimous, at least, in that respect. If this truth had been as necessary as the sun is to the earth, it would have been as brilliant as that planet. It is an absurdity, an insult to human nature—it is an attack upon the Infinite and Supreme

Being to say there is a truth essential to the happiness of man which God conceals."

All that this ignorant youth, instructed only by nature, said, made a very deep impression upon the mind of the old unhappy scholiast.

"Is it really certain," he cried, "that I should have made myself truly miserable for mere chimeras? I am much more certain of my misery than of effectual grace. I have spent my time in reasoning about the liberty of God and human nature, but I have lost my own. Neither St. Augustine nor St Prosner will extricate me from my present misfortunes."

The ingenuous Huron, who gave way to his natural instincts, at length said:

"Will you give me leave to speak to you boldly and frankly? Those who bring upon themselves persecution for such idle disputes seem to me to have very little sense; those who persecute, appear to me very monsters."

The two captives entirely coincided with respect to the injustice of their captivity.

"I am a hundred times more to be pitied than you," said the Huron; "I am born free as the air: I had two lives, liberty and the object of my love; and I am deprived of both. We are both in fetters, without knowing who put them on us, or without being able to inquire. It is said that the Hurons are barbarians, because they avenge themselves on their enemies; but they never oppress their friends. I had scarce set foot in France, before I shed my blood for this country. I have, perhaps, preserved a whole province, and my recompense is imprisonment. In this country men are condemned without being heard. This is not the case in England. Alas! it was not against the English that I should have fought."

Thus his growing philosophy could not brook nature being insulted in the first of her rights, and he gave vent to his just indignation.

His companion did not contradict him. Absence ever increases ungratified love, and philosophy does not diminish it. He as frequently spoke of his dear Miss St. Yves, as he did of morality or metaphysics. The more he purified his sentiments, the more he loved. He read some new romances; but he met with few that depicted to him the real state of his soul. He felt that his heart stretched beyond the bounds of his author.

"Alas!" said he, "almost all these writers have nothing but wit and art."

At length, the good Jansenist became, insensibly, the confidant of his tenderness. He was already acquainted with love as a sin with which a penitent accuses himself at confession. He now learned to know it as a sentiment equally noble and tender; which can elevate the soul as well as soften it, and can at times produce virtues. In fine, for the last miracle, a Huron converted a Jansenist.

CHAPTER XV

The Beautiful Miss St. Yves Visits M. de St. Pouange

THE CHARMING MISS ST. YVES, STILL MORE AFFLICTED THAN HER lover, waited accordingly upon M. de St. Pouange, accompanied by her friend with whom she lodged, each having their faces covered with their hoods. The first thing she saw at the door was the Abbé St. Yves, her brother, coming out. She was terrified, but her friend supported her spirits.

"For the very reason," said she, "that people have been speaking against you, speak to him for yourself. You may be assured, that the accusers in this part of the world are always in the right, unless they are immediately detected. Besides, your presence will have greater effect, or else I am much mistaken, than the words of your brother."

Ever so little encouragement to a passionate lover makes her intrepid. Miss St. Yves appears at the audience. Her youth, her charms, her languishing eyes, moistened with some involuntary tears, attract everyone's attention. Every sycophant to the deputy minister forgot for an instant the idol of power to contemplate that of beauty. St. Pouange conducted her into a closet. She spoke with an affecting grace. St. Pouange felt some emotion. She trembled, but he told her not to be afraid.

"Return to-night," said he; "your business requires some reflection, and it must be discussed at leisure. There are too many people here at present. Audiences are rapidly dispatched. I must get to the bottom of all that concerns you."

He then paid her some compliments upon her beauty and address, and advised her to come at seven in the evening.

She did not fail attending at the hour appointed, and her pious friend again accompanied her; but she remained in the hall, where she read whilst St. Pouange and the beauteous Miss St. Yves were in the back closet. He began by saying:

"Would you believe it, Miss, that your brother has been to request me to grant him a *lettre de cachet* against you; but, indeed, I would sooner grant one to send him back to Lower Brittany."

"Alas! sir," said she, "*lettres de cachet* are granted very liberally in your offices, since people come from the extremity of the kingdom to solicit them like pensions. I am very far from requesting one against my brother, yet I have much reason to complain of him. But I respect the liberty of mankind; and, therefore, supplicate for that of a man whom I want to make my husband; of a man to whom the king is indebted for the preservation of a province; who can beneficially serve him; and who is the son of an officer killed in his service. Of what is he accused? How could he be treated so cruelly without being heard?"

The deputy minister then showed her the letter of the spy, and that of the perfidious bailiff.

"What!" said she with astonishment, "are there such monsters upon earth? and would they force me to marry the stupid son of a ridiculous, wicked man? and is it upon such evidence that the fate of citizens is determined?"

She threw herself upon her knees, and with a flood of tears solicited the freedom of a brave man who adored her. Her charms appeared to the greatest advantage in such a situation. She was so beautiful, that St. Pouange, bereft of all shame, used words with some reserve, which brought on others less delicate, which were succeeded by those still more expressive. The revocation of the *lettre de cachet* was proposed, and he at length went so far as to state the only means of obtaining the liberty of the man whose interest she had so violently and affectionately at heart.

This uncommon conversation continued for a long time. The devotee in the ante-chamber said to herself:

"My lord St. Pouange never before gave so long an audience. Perhaps he has refused everything to this poor girl, and she is still entreating him."

At length her companion came out of the closet in the greatest confusion, without being able to speak. She was lost in deep meditation upon the character of the great and the half great, who so slightly sacrifice the liberty of men and the honor of women.

She did not utter a syllable all the way back. But having returned to her friend's she burst out, and told all that had happened. Her pious friend made frequent signs of the cross.

"My dear friend," said she, "you must consult to-morrow *Tout-a-tous,* our director. He has much influence over M. de St. Pouange. Yield to him; this is my way; and I always found myself right. We weak women stand in need of a man to lead us: and so, my dear friend, I'll go tomorrow in search of *Tout-a-tous.*"

CHAPTER XVI

Miss St. Yves Consults a Cleric

No sooner was the beautiful and disconsolate Miss St. Yves with her director than she told him, "that a powerful, voluptuous man, had proposed to her to set at liberty the man whom she intended making her lawful husband, and that he required a great price for his service; that she held such infidelity in the highest detestation; and that if her life only had been required, she would much sooner have sacrificed it than to have submitted."

"This is a most abominable sinner," said *Tout-a-tous.* "You should tell me the name of this vile man. He must certainly be some Jansenist. I will inform against him to the king's adviser, who will place him in the situation of your dear beloved intended bridegroom."

The poor girl, after much hesitation and embarrassment, at length mentioned St. Pouange.

"My Lord St. Pouange!" cried the cleric. "Ah! my child, the case is quite different. He is cousin to the greatest minister we have ever had; a man of worth, a protector of the good cause, a good Christian. He could not entertain such a thought. You certainly must have misunderstood him."

"Oh! I did but understand him too well. I am lost on whichever side I turn. The only alternative I have to choose is misery or shame; either my lover must be buried alive, or I must make myself unworthy of living. I cannot let him perish, nor can I save him."

Tout-a-tous endeavored to console her with these gentle expressions:

"In the *first place,* my child, never use the word lover. It intimates something worldly, which may offend God. Say my husband. You consider him as such, and nothing can be more decent.

"*Secondly*: Though he be ideally your husband, and you are in hopes he will be such eventually, yet he is not so in reality.

"*Thirdly*: Actions are not maliciously culpable, when the intention is virtuous; and nothing can be more virtuous than to procure your husband his liberty."

The beautiful Miss St. Yves, who was no less terrified with the cleric's discourse than with the proposals of the deputy minister, returned in despair to her friend. She was tempted to deliver herself by death from the horror of her situation.

CHAPTER XVII

The Cleric Triumphs

The unfortunate Miss St. Yves entreated her friend to kill her; but this lady, who was fully as indulgent as the cleric, spoke to her still more clearly.

"Alas!" said she, "at this agreeable, gallant, and famous court, business is always thus transacted. The most considerable, as well as the most indifferent places are seldom given away without a consideration. The dignities of war are solicited by the queen of love, and, without regard to merit, a place is often given to him who has the handsomest advocate."

"You are in a situation that is extremely critical. The object is to restore your lover to liberty, and to marry him. It is a sacred duty that you are to fulfill. The world will applaud you. It will be said, that you only allowed yourself to be guilty of a weakness, through an excess of virtue."

"Heavens!" cried Miss St. Yves. "What kind of virtue is this? What a labyrinth of distress! What a world! What men to become acquainted with! A king's adviser and a ridiculous bailiff imprison my lover; I am persecuted by my family; assistance is offered me, only that I may be dishonored! A cleric has ruined a brave man, another wants to ruin me. On every side snares are laid for me, and I am upon the very brink of destruction! I must even speak to the king; I will throw myself at his feet as he goes to mass or to the theatre."

"His attendants will not let you approach," said her good friend; "and if you should be so unfortunate as to speak to him, M. de Louvois, or the king's adviser might bury you in a convent for the rest of your days."

Whilst this generous friend thus increased the perplexities of Miss St. Yves's tortured soul, and plunged the dagger deeper in her heart, a messenger arrived from M. de St. Pouange with a letter, and two fine pendant earrings. Miss St. Yves, with tears, refused to accept of any part of the contents of the packet; but her friend took the charge of them upon herself.

As soon as the messenger had gone, the *confidante* read the letter, in which a *petit-souper* (a little supper) was proposed to the two friends for that night. Miss St. Yves protested she would not go, whilst her pious friend endeavored to make her try on the diamond earrings; but Miss St. Yves could not endure them, and opposed it all the day long; being entirely wrapped up in the contemplation of her lover's imprisonment. At length, after a long resistance—after sighs, moans, and torrents of tears—driven by excitement almost to the verge of insanity—weakened with the conflict, overwhelmed and irresolute, the innocent victim, not knowing whether she was going, was dragged by this artful woman to the fatal supper of the "good Christian and protector of the good cause," M. de St. Pouange.

CHAPTER XVIII

Miss St. Yves Delivers Her Lover and a Jansenist

At day-break she fled to Paris with the minister's mandate. It would be difficult to depict the agitation of her mind in this journey. Imagine a virtuous and noble soul, humbled by its own reproaches, intoxicated with tenderness, distracted with the remorse of having betrayed her lover, and elated with the pleasure of releasing the object of her adoration. Her torments and conflicts by turns engaged her reflections. She was no longer that innocent girl whose ideas were confined to a provincial education. Love and misfortunes had united to remould her. Sentiment had made as rapid a progress in her mind, as reason had in that of her lover.

Her dress was dictated by the greatest simplicity. She viewed with horror the trappings with which she had appeared before her fatal benefactor. Her companion had taken the earrings without her having looked at them. Anxious and confused, idolizing the Huron and detesting herself, she at length arrived at the gate of that dreadful castle—the palace of vengeance—where crimes and innocence are alike immured.

When she was upon the point of getting out of the coach her strength failed her. Some people came to her assistance. She entered, whilst her heart was in the greatest palpitation, her eyes streaming, and her whole frame bespoke the greatest consternation. She was presented to the governor. He was going to speak to her, but she had lost all power of expression: she showed her order, whilst, with great difficulty, she articulated some accents. The governor entertained a great esteem for his prisoner, and he was greatly pleased at his being released. His heart was not callous, like those of most of his brethren, who think of nothing but the fees their captives are to pay them; extort their revenues from their victims; and living by the misery of others, conceive a horrid joy at the lamentations of the unfortunate.

He sent for the prisoner into his apartment. The two lovers swooned at the sight of each other. The beautiful Miss St. Yves remained for a long time motionless, without any symptoms of life; the other soon recalled his fortitude.

"This lady," said the governor, "is probably your wife. You did not tell me you were married. I am informed that it is through her generous solicitude that you have obtained your liberty."

"Alas!" said the beautiful Miss St. Yves, in a faltering voice, "I am not worthy of being his wife"; and swooned again.

When she recovered her senses, she presented, with a trembling hand and averted eyes, the grant and written promise of a company.

The Huron, equally astonished and affected, awoke from one dream to fall into another.

"Why was I shut up here? How could you deliver me? Where are the monsters that immured me? You are a divinity sent from heaven to succor me."

The beautiful Miss St. Yves, with a dejected air, looked at her lover, blushed, and instantly turned away her streaming eyes. In a word, they told him all she knew, and all she had undergone, except what she was willing to conceal forever, but which any other than the Huron, more accustomed to the world and better acquainted with the customs of courts, would easily have guessed.

"Is it possible." said he, "that a wretch like the bailiff can have deprived me of my liberty?

"Alas! I find that men, like the vilest of animals, can all injure.

"But is it possible that a cleric, the king's adviser, should have contributed to my misfortunes as much as the bailiff, without my being able to imagine under what pretence this detestable knave has persecuted me? Did he make me pass for a Jansenist? In fine, how came you to remember me? I did not deserve it; I was then only a savage.

"What! could you, without advice, without assistance, undertake a journey to Versailles?

"You there appeared, and my fetters were broken!

"There must then be in beauty and virtue an invincible charm, that opens gates of adamant and softens hearts of steel."

At the word virtue, a flood of tears issued from the eyes of the beautiful Miss St. Yves. She did not know how far she had been virtuous in the crime with which she reproached herself.

Her lover thus continued:

"Thou angel, who hast broken my chains, if thou hast had sufficient influence (which I cannot yet comprehend) to obtain justice for me, obtain it likewise for an old man who first taught me to think, as thou didst to love. Misfortunes have united us; I love him as a father; I can neither live without thee nor him."

"I solicit?"

"The same man."

"Who!"

"Yes, I will be beholden to you for everything, and I will owe nothing to anyone but yourself. Write to this man in power. Overwhelm me with kindness—complete what you have begun—perfect your miracle."

She was sensible she ought to do everything her lover desired. She wanted to write, but her hand refused its office. She began her letter three times and tore it as often. At length she got to the end, and the two lovers left the prison, after having embraced the old martyr to efficacious grace.

The happy yet disconsolate Miss St. Yves knew where her brother lodged: thither she repaired; and her lover took an apartment at the same house.

They had scarce reached their lodging, before her protector sent the order for releasing the good old Gordon, at the same time making an appointment with her for the next day.

She gave the order of release to her lover, and refused the appointment of a benefactor whom she could no more see without expiring with shame and grief.

Her lover would not have left her upon any other errand than to release his friend. He flew to the place of his confinement and fulfilled this duty, reflecting, meanwhile, upon the strange vicissitudes of this world, and admiring the courageous virtue of a young lady, to whom two unfortunate men owed more than life.

CHAPTER XIX

The Huron, the Beautiful Miss St. Yves, and Their Relations Are Convened

THE GENEROUS AND RESPECTABLE, BUT INJURED GIRL, WAS WITH her brother the Abbé de St. Yves, the good Prior of the Mountain, and Lady de Kerkabon. They were equally astonished, but their situations and sentiments were very different. The Abbé de St. Yves was expiating the wrongs he had done his sister at her feet, and she pardoned him. The Prior and his sympathizing sister likewise wept, but it was for joy. The filthy bailiff and his insupportable son did not trouble this affecting scene. They had set out upon the first report that their antagonist had been released. They flew to bury in their own province their folly and fear.

The four *dramatis personae*, variously agitated, were waiting for the return of the young man who had gone to deliver his friend. The Abbé de St. Yves did not dare to raise his eyes to meet those of his sister. The good Kerkabon said:

"I shall then see once more my dear nephew."

"You will see him again," said the charming Miss St. Yves, "but he is no longer the same man. His behavior, his manners, his ideas, his sense, have all undergone a complete mutation. He has become as respectable, as he was before ignorant and strange to everything. He will be the honor and consolation of your family; would to heaven that I might also be the honor of mine!"

"What, are you not the same as you were?" said the Prior. "What then has happened to work so great a change?"

During this conversation the Huron returned in company with the Jansenist. The scene was now changed, and became more interesting. It began by the uncle and aunt's tender embraces. The Abbé de St. Yves almost kissed the knees of the ingenuous Huron, who, by the by, was no longer ingenuous. The language of the eyes formed all the discourse of the two lovers, who, nevertheless, expressed every sentiment with which they were penetrated. Satisfaction and acknowledgment sparkled in the countenance of the one, whilst embarrassment was depicted in Miss St. Yves's melting but half averted eyes. Everyone was astonished that she should mingle grief with so much joy.

The venerable Gordon soon endeared himself to the whole family. He had been unhappy with the young prisoner, and this was a sufficient title to their esteem. He owed his deliverance to the two lovers, and this alone reconciled him to love. The acrimony of his former sentiments was dismissed from his heart—he was converted by gratitude, as well as the Huron. Everyone related his adventures before supper. The two Abbés and the aunt listened like children to the relation of stories of ghosts, and both were deeply interested.

"Alas!" said Gordon, "there are perhaps upwards of five hundred virtuous people in the same fetters as Miss St. Yves has broken. Their misfortunes are unheeded. Many hands are found to strike the unhappy multitude,—how seldom one to succor them."

This very just reflection increased his sensibility and gratitude. Everything heightened the triumph of the beautiful Miss St. Yves. The grandeur and intrepidity of her soul were the subject of each one's admiration. This admiration was blended with that respect which we feel in spite of ourselves for a person who we think has some influence at court. But the Abbé de St. Yves inquired:

"What could my sister do to obtain this influence so soon?"

Supper being ready, everyone was already seated, when, lo! the worthy *confidante* of Versailles arrived, without being acquainted with anything that had passed. She was in a coach and six, and it was easily seen to whom the equipage belonged. She entered with that air of authority assumed by people in power who have a great deal of business—saluted the company with much indifference, and, pulling the beautiful Miss St. Yves on one side, said:

"Why do you make people wait so long? Follow me. There are the diamonds you forgot."

However softly she uttered these expressions, the Huron, nevertheless, overheard them. He saw the diamonds. The brother was speechless. The uncle and aunt exhibited the surprise of good people, who had never before beheld such magnificence. The young man, whose mind was now formed by an experience of twelve months, could not help making some reflections against his will, and was for a moment in anxiety. His mistress perceived it, and a mortal paleness spread itself over her countenance; a tremor seized her, and it was with difficulty she could support herself.

"Ah! madam," said she to her fatal friend, "you have ruined me—you have given me the mortal blow."

These words pierced the heart of the Huron: but he had already learned to possess himself. He did not dwell upon them, lest he should make his mistress uneasy before her brother, but turned pale as well as she.

Miss St. Yves, distracted with the change she perceived in her lover's countenance, pulled the woman out of the room into the passage, and there threw the jewels at her feet, saying:

"Alas! these were not my seducers, as you well know: but he that gave them shall never set eyes on me again."

Her friend took them up, whilst Miss St. Yves added:

"He may either take them again, or give them to you. Begone, and do not make me still more odious to myself."

The ambassadress at length departed, not being able to comprehend the remorse to which she had been witness.

The beautiful Miss St. Yves, greatly oppressed and feeling a revolution in her body that almost suffocated her, was compelled to go to bed; but that she might not alarm anyone she kept her pains and sufferings to herself: and under pretence of only being weary, she asked leave to take a little rest. This, however, she did not do till she had reanimated the company with consolatory and flattering expressions, and cast such a kind look upon her lover as darted fire into his soul.

The supper, of which she did not partake, was in the beginning gloomy; but this gloominess was of that interesting kind which inspires reflection and useful conversation, so superior to that frivolous excitement commonly exhibited, and which is usually nothing more than a troublesome noise.

Gordon, in a few words, gave the history of Jansenism and Molinism; of those persecutions with which one party hampered the other; and of the obstinacy of both. The Huron entered into a criticism thereupon, pitying those men who, not satisfied with all the confusion occasioned by these opposite interests, create evils by imaginary interests and unintelligible absurdities. Gordon related—the other judged. The guests listened with emotion, and gained new lights. The duration of misfortunes, and the shortness of life, then became the topics. It was remarked that all professions have peculiar vices and dangers annexed to them; and that from the prince down to the lowest beggar, all seemed alike to accuse providence. How happens it that so many men, for so little, perform the office of persecutors, sergeants, and executioners, to others? With what inhuman indifference does a man in authority sign papers for the destruction of a family; and with what joy, still more barbarous, do mercenaries execute them.

"I saw in my youth," said the good old Gordon, "a relation of the Marshal de Marillic, who, being prosecuted in his own province on account of that illustrious but unfortunate man, concealed himself under a borrowed name in Paris. He was an old man near seventy-two years of age. His wife, who accompanied him, was nearly of the same age. They had a libertine son, who at fourteen years of age absconded from his father's house, turned soldier, and deserted. He had gone through every gradation of debauchery and misery: at length having changed his name, he was in the guards of the king and had obtained an exempt's staff in their company of sergeants.

"This adventurer was appointed to arrest the old man and his wife, and acquitted himself with all the obduracy of a man who was willing to please his master. As he was conducting them, he heard these two victims deplore the long succession of miseries which had befallen them from their cradle. This aged couple reckoned as one of their greatest misfortunes the wildness and loss of their son. He recollected them, but he nevertheless led them to prison; assuring them, that the king was to be served in preference to everybody else. His Highness rewarded his zeal.

"I have seen a spy of the king's adviser betray his own brother, in hopes of a little benefice, which he did not obtain; and I saw him die, not of remorse, but of grief at having been cheated by the man.

"The vocation of an adviser, which I for a long while exercised, made me acquainted with the secrets of families. I have known very few, who, though immersed in the greatest distress, did not externally wear the mask of felicity and every appearance of joy; and I have always observed that great grief was the fruit of our unconstrained desires."

"For my part," said the Huron, "I imagine, that a noble, grateful, sensible man, may always be happy; and I hope to enjoy an uncheckered felicity with the charming, generous Miss St. Yves. For I flatter myself," added he, in addressing himself to her brother with a friendly smile, "that you will not now refuse me as you did last year: besides, I shall pursue a more decent method."

The Abbé was confounded in apologies for the past, and in protesting an eternal attachment.

Uncle Kerkabon said this would be the most glorious day of his whole life. His good aunt Kerkabon, in ecstasies of joy, cried out:

"I always said you would never be a sub-deacon.

And now all vied with each other in applauding the gentle Miss St. Yves.

Her lover's heart was too full of what she had done for him, and he loved her too much, for the affair of the jewels to make any permanent impression on him. But those words, which he too well heard, "*you have given me the mortal blow,*" still secretly terrified him, and interrupted all his joy; whilst the eulogiums paid his beautiful mistress still increased his love. In a word, nothing was thought of but her,—nothing was mentioned but the happiness those two lovers deserved. A plan was agitated to live altogether at Paris, and schemes of grandeur and fortune were formed. These hopes, which the smallest ray of happiness engenders, were predominant. But the Huron felt, in the secret recesses of his heart, a sentiment that exploded the illusion. He read over the promises signed by St. Pouange, and the commission signed Louvois. These men were painted to him such as they were or such as they were thought to be. Everyone spoke of the ministers and administration with the freedom of convivial conversation, which is considered in France as the most precious liberty to be obtained on earth.

"If I were king of France," said the Huron, "this is the kind of minister that I would choose for the war department. I would have a man of the highest birth, as he is to give orders to the nobility. I would require that he should himself have been an officer, and have passed through the various gradations; or, at least, that he had attained the rank of Lieutenant General, and was worthy of being a Marshal of France. For, to be acquainted with the details of the service, is it not necessary that he himself should have served? and will not officers obey, with a hundred times more alacrity, a military man, who like themselves has been signalized by his courage, rather than a mere man of the cabinet, who, whatever natural ability he may possess, can, at most, only guess at the operations of a campaign? I should not be displeased at my minister's generosity, even though it might sometimes embarrass a little the keeper of the royal treasure. I should desire him to have a facility in business, and that he should distinguish himself by that kind of gaiety of mind, which is the lot of men superior to business, which is so agreeable to the nation, and which renders the performance of every duty less irksome."

This is the character he would have chosen for a minister, as he had constantly observed that such an amiable disposition is incompatible with cruelty.

Monsieur de Louvois would not, perhaps, have been satisfied with the Huron's wishes. His merit lay in a different walk. But whilst they were still at table, the disorder of the unhappy Miss

St. Yves took a fatal turn. Her blood was on fire,—the symptoms of a malignant fever had appeared. She suffered, but did not complain, being unwilling to disturb the pleasure of the guests.

Her brother, thinking that she was not asleep, went to the foot of her bed. He was astonished at the condition he found her in. Everybody flew to her. Her lover appeared next to her brother. He was certainly the most alarmed, and the most affected of anyone; but he had learned to unite discretion to all the happy gifts nature had bestowed upon him, and a quick sensibility of decorum began to prevail over him.

A neighboring physician was immediately sent for. He was one of those itinerant doctors who confound the last disorder they were consulted upon with the present;—who follow a blind practice in a science from which the most mature investigations and careful observations do not preclude uncertainty and danger. He greatly increased the disorder by prescribing a fashionable nostrum. Can fashion extend to medicine? This frenzy was then too prevalent in Paris.

The grief of Miss St. Yves contributed still more than her physician to render her disorder fatal. Her body suffered martyrdom in the torments of her mind. The crowd of thoughts which agitated her breast, communicated to her veins a more dangerous poison than that of the most burning fever.

CHAPTER XX

The Death of the Beautiful Miss St. Yves and Its Consequences

ANOTHER PHYSICIAN WAS CALLED IN. BUT, INSTEAD OF ASSISTING nature and leaving it to act in a young person whose organs recalled the vital stream, he applied himself solely to counteract the effects of his brother's prescription. The disorder, in two days, became mortal. The brain, which is thought to be the seat of the mind, was as violently affected as the heart, which, we are told, is the seat of the passions. By what incomprehensible mechanism are our organs held in subjection to sentiment and thought? How is it that a single melancholy idea shall disturb the whole course of the blood; and that the blood should in turn communicate irregularities to the human understanding? What is that unknown fluid which certainly exists and which, quicker and more active than light, flies in less than the twinkling of an eye into all the channels of life,—produces sensations, memory, joy or grief, reason or frenzy,—recalls with horror what we would choose to forget; and renders a thinking animal, either a subject of admiration, or an object of pity and compassion?

These were the reflections of the good old Gordon; and these observations, so natural, which men seldom make, did not prevent his feeling upon this occasion; for he was not of the number of those gloomy philosophers who pique themselves upon being insensible.

He was affected at the fate of this young woman, like a father who sees his dear child yielding to a slow death. The Abbé de St. Yves was desperate; the Prior and his sister shed floods of tears; but who could describe the situation of her lover? All expression falls far short of the intensity of his affliction.

His aunt, almost lifeless, supported the head of the departing fair in her feeble arms; her brother was upon his knees at the foot of the bed; her lover squeezed her hand, which he bathed in tears; his groans rent the air, whilst he called her his guardian angel, his life, his hope, his better half, his mistress, his wife. At the word wife, a sigh escaped her, whilst she looked upon him with inexpressible tenderness, and then abruptly gave a horrid scream. Presently in one of those intervals when brief, the oppression of the senses, and pain subside and leave the soul its liberty and powers, she cried out:

"I your wife? Ah! dear lover, this name, this happiness, this felicity, were not destined for me! I die, and I deserve it. O idol of my heart! O you, whom I sacrificed to infernal demons—it is done—I am punished—live and be happy!"

These tender but dreadful expressions were incomprehensible; yet they melted and terrified every heart. She had the courage to explain herself, and her auditors quaked with astonishment, grief, and pity. They with one voice detested the man in power, who repaired a shocking act of injustice only by his crimes, and who had forced the most amiable innocence to be his accomplice.

"Who? you guilty?" said her lover, "no, you are not. Guilt can only be in the heart;—yours is devoted solely to virtue and to me."

This opinion he corroborated by such expressions as seemed to recall the beautiful Miss St. Yves back to life. She felt some consolation from them and was astonished at being still beloved. The aged Gordon would have condemned her at the time he was only a Jansenist; but having attained wisdom, he esteemed her, and wept.

In the midst of these lamentations and fears, whilst the dangerous situation of this worthy girl engrossed every breast, and all were in the greatest consternation, a courier arrived from court.

"A courier? from whom, and upon what account?"

He was sent by the king's adviser to the Prior of the Mountain.

He wrote to the Abbé of the Mountain, "that had been informed of his nephew's exploits: that his being sent to prison was through mistake; that such little accidents frequently happened, and should therefore not be attended to; and, in fine, it behoved him, the Prior, to come and present his nephew the next day: that he was to bring with him that good man Gordon; and that he should introduce them to M. de Louvois, who would say a word to them in his ante-chamber."

To which he added, "that the history of the Huron, and his combat against the English, had been related to the king; that doubtless the king would deign to take notice of him in passing through the gallery, and perhaps he might even nod his head to him."

The letter concluded by flattering him with hopes that all the ladies of the court would show their eagerness to recognize his nephew; and that several among them would say to him, "Good day, Mr. Huron;" and that he would certainly be talked of at the king's supper.

The Prior having read the letter aloud, his furious nephew for an instant suppressed his rage, and said nothing to the bearer: but turning toward the companion of his misfortunes, asked him, what he thought of that communication? Gordon replied:

"This, then, is the way that men are treated! They are first beaten and then, like monkeys, they dance."

The Huron resuming his character, which always returned in the great emotions of his soul, tore the letter to bits, and threw them in the courier's face:

"There is my answer," said he.

His uncle was in terror, and fancied he saw thunderbolts, and twenty *lettres de cachet* at once fall upon him. He immediately wrote the best excuse he could for these transports of passion in a young man, which he considered as the ebullition of a great soul.

But a solicitude of a more melancholy stamp now seized every heart. The beautiful and unfortunate Miss St. Yves was already sensible of her approaching end; she was serene, but it was that kind of shocking serenity, the result of exhausted nature being no longer able to withstand the conflict.

"Oh, my dear lover!" said she, in a faltering voice, "death punishes me for my weakness; but I expire with the consolation of knowing you are free. I adored you whilst I betrayed you, and I adore you in bidding you an eternal adieu."

She did not make a parade of a ridiculous fortitude; she did not understand that miserable glory of having some of her neighbors say, "she died with courage." Who, at twenty, can be at once torn from her lover, from life, and what is called honor, without regret, without some pangs? She felt all the horror of her situation, and made it felt by those expiring looks and accents which speak with so much energy. In a word, she shed tears like other people at those intervals that she was capable of giving vent to them.

Let others strive to celebrate the pompous deaths of those who insensibly rush into destruction. This is the lot of all animals. We die like them only when age or disorders make us resemble them by the paralysis of our organs. Whoever suffers a great loss must feel great regrets. If they are stifled, it is nothing but vanity that is pursued, even in the arms of death.

When the fatal moment came, all around her most feelingly expressed their grief by incessant tears and lamentations. The Huron was senseless. Great souls feel more violent sensations than those of less tender dispositions. The good old Gordon knew enough of his companion to dread that when he came to himself he would be guilty of suicide. All kinds of arms were put out of his way, which the unfortunate young man perceived. He said to his relations and Gordon, without shedding any tears, without a groan, or the least emotion:

"Do you then think that anyone upon earth hath the right and power to prevent my putting an end to my life?"

Gordon took care to avoid making a parade of those commonplace declamations and arguments which are relied on to prove that we are not allowed to exercise our liberty in ceasing to be when we are in a wretched situation; that we should not leave the house when we can no longer remain in it; that a man is like a soldier at his post; as if it signified to the Being of beings whether the conjunction of the particles of matter were in one spot or another. Impotent reasons, to which a firm and concentrated despair disdains to listen, and to which Cato replied only with the use of a poniard.

The Huron's sullen and dreadful silence, his doleful aspect, his trembling lips, and the shivering of his whole frame, communicated to every spectator's soul that mixture of compassion and terror, which fetters all our powers, precludes discourse, or compels us to speak only in faltering accents. The hostess and her family were excited. They trembled to behold the state of his desperation, yet all kept their eyes upon him, and attended to all his motions. The ice-cold corpse of the beautiful Miss St. Yves had already been carried into a lower hall out of the sight of her lover, who seemed still in search of it, though incapable of observing any object.

In the midst of this spectacle of death, whilst the dead body was exposed at the door of the house; whilst her relations were drowned in tears, and everyone thought the lover would not survive his loss;—in this situation St. Pouange arrived with his female Versailles friend.

He alighted from his coach; and the first object that presented itself was a bier: he turned away his eyes with that simple distaste of a man bred up in pleasures, and who thinks he should avoid a spectacle which might recall him to the contemplation of human misery. He is inclined to go upstairs, whilst his female friend inquires through curiosity whose funeral it is. The name of Miss St. Yves is pronounced. At this name she turned, and gave a piercing shriek. St. Pouange now returns, whilst surprise and grief possess his soul. The good old Gordon stood with streaming eyes. He for a moment ceased his lamentations, to acquaint the courtier with all the circumstances of this melancholy catastrophe. He spoke with that authority which is the companion to sorrow and virtue. St. Pouange was not naturally wicked. The torrent of business and amusements had hurried away his soul, which was not yet acquainted with itself. He did not border upon that grey age which usually hardens the hearts of ministers. He listened to Gordon with a downcast look, and some tears escaped him, which he was surprised to shed. In a word, he repented.

"I will," said he, "absolutely see this extraordinary man you have mentioned to me. He affects me almost as much as this innocent victim, whose death I have occasioned."

Gordon followed him as far as the chamber in which the Prior Kerkabon, the Abbé St. Yves, and some neighbors, were striving to recall to life the young man, who had again fainted.

"I have been the cause of your misfortunes," said the deputy minister, when the Huron had regained consciousness, "and my whole life shall be employed in making reparation for my error."

The first idea that struck the Huron was to kill him and then destroy himself. But he was without arms, and closely watched. St. Pouange was not repulsed with refusals accompanied with reproach, contempt, and the insults he deserved, which were lavished upon him. Time softens everything. Mons. de Louvois at length succeeded in making an excellent officer of the Huron, who has appeared under another name at Paris and in the army, respected by all honest men, being at once a warrior and an intrepid philosopher.

He never mentioned this adventure without being greatly affected, and yet his greatest consolation was to speak of it. He cherished the memory of his beloved Miss St. Yves to the last moment of his life.

The Abbé St. Yves and the Prior were each provided with good livings. The good Kerkabon rather chose to see his nephew invested with military honors than in the sub-deaconry. The devotee of Versailles kept the diamond earrings, and received besides a handsome present. *Tout-a-tous* had presents of chocolate, coffee, and confectionery. Good old Gordon lived with the Huron till his death, in the most friendly intimacy: he had also a benefice, and forgot, forever, essential grace, and the concomitant concourse. He took for his motto, "Misfortunes are of some use." How many worthy people are there in the world who may justly say, "Misfortunes are good for nothing?"